The Call of Tawiskaro

& Other Tales of Woe and Whimsy

T. W. Kriner

J & J Publishing

ISBN 978-0-9657245-6-2

Produced by:

J & J Publishing
P. O. Box 643
Buffalo, New York 14231

for Frank Barcaro

CONTENTS

THE ONE WAY

William Jenison inspected his face in the mirror of the makeup kit. Satisfied, he took off his Grateful Dead t–shirt and used it to wipe the greasepaint from his hands. He dropped the kit and soiled shirt into a trash barrel. He walked over the sun–bleached grass toward the air show spectators crowding the tarmac where the C5–B Galaxy was parked. Most of the people he brushed by were gazing at the huge Air Force transport, waiting for its taxi and takeoff. Those who noticed him cast startled glances at his face and disfigured torso, and quickly stepped out of the way.

Jenison was six feet tall. His black hair hung down to his shoulders. Below that he was tanned and scarred. Patches of thick pink scar tissue wound from his belly to his back. Tiny disks of white flesh dotted his chest and shoulders. A pale keloid ring circled his neck like a collar. He had painted the right half of his face bone white and the left black, from hairline to throat. A lopsided red smile stretched from ear to ear.

He worked his way to the fence that kept spectators out of the flight operations area, opposite the towering nose of the Galaxy, and stood between an old man with a parasol and a fat woman wearing a baseball cap. He scanned the tarmac perimeter. There were only six Air Force Security Forces airmen: four men spaced along the fence for crowd control and two near the hangar wall behind the plane. Fifty yards in front of the Galaxy, a signalman stood ready to direct the pilot to the main runway. A yellow fuel truck rolled slowly away from the tail of the plane In a wide arc that would carry it around the port wing, toward the crowd. The driver craned his neck as he made a final walk around inspection. The Galaxy's four turbofans whined toward a continuous shriek as their shafts approached takeoff revolutions.

Jenison needed one of those engines. His research had convinced him that the forty–one thousand pounds of thrust produced by such a turbine would provide the means to escape Flint. But he hadn't expected it to be this easy, not even at the Niagara Falls Air Reserve Station; security was light and out of position to interfere, and the fuel truck he would use to access the engine was coming right to him.

He grasped the steel crossbar of the chain link fence as the vehicle approached. He was about to vault over the barrier when someone grabbed his left shoulder. He turned and reflexively swept his arm up and back to break the grip, but stopped when he saw that it was only the old man with the parasol. Jenison had expected to see an Air Force uniform, not this wizened stranger. He peered at the wrinkled face in the shadow of the umbrella and a thrill of fear shot from his stomach to his throat. He didn't know the man, but he recognized the look.

"Enjoying the air show, Deoneyont?" The old man's eyes were fixed in a bulging stare. His jaw moved woodenly like that of a ventriloquist's dummy. The Thunderbirds were most Impressive, don't you think?"

"*You.*" Jenison pushed the thin arm away and glanced anxiously over his shoulder as the fuel truck moved slowly by.

"Don't worry. There is plenty of time."

"It's over, demon." Jenison said. He forced a smile. "I'm rid of you."

"We shall see." The old man's eyes narrowed to slits. "You've chosen a False Face for the occasion. Is it one of the

2

doorkeepers? No. No, they do not split their faces." He grinned suddenly—a toothy rictus that didn't quite match his weathered features. "It's the mask of Thagonhsowes, isn't it? How appropriate!"

"Goodbye, demon."

"You will fail," the old man shouted as Jenison sprang over the fence and began to run. "This is not the One Way!"

If the old man said anything else Jenison couldn't hear it over the building roar of the Galaxy's engines. It didn't matter. The creature was a liar. This was the One Way—he was sure of it. This time he would succeed.

He ran straight across the tarmac to intercept the fuel truck as it circled toward the Galaxy's starboard wing. The course he selected led him to the signalman. At the last moment he lowered his head and rammed his shoulder into the middle of the man's back. The impact knocked the barracks cap and ear protectors from the signalman's head and smashed his body to the ground in a heap. Jenison stumbled over him, but was quickly running again, and caught up with the truck at a point thirty yards equidistant from the plane's nose and wing tip. He jumped up onto the running board and yanked open the passenger door. The driver directed a look of astonishment at him as he gripped the door frame and swung into the cab feet first. He thrust his heels into the man's face and felt the crunch of snapping cartilage. After braking the truck he dragged the limp body to the ground.

Jenison looked down the length of the Galaxy and saw two airmen running toward him. They hadn't reached the tail of the plane yet. Of more concern were the four men who had been positioned along the fence. They must be close by now. He climbed back into the cab and cut the wheel hard to the left. He backed up, then shifted into first gear and accelerated. His pursuers had been slow to react. They were just now converging on the signalman. Jenison shifted into second gear and drove around the fallen man, steering directly for the nearest cop, who immediately dropped his baton and sprinted for the runway without looking back. The remaining men retreated toward the crowd as he threatened each in turn.

Satisfied that they had given up the chase, Jenison spun the wheel back to the right and drove to the Galaxy's port wing. He aligned the truck's fuel container with the outboard engine and parked with the cab directly below the turbofan.

The one hundred decibel shriek of the engine made Jenison's teeth sing. His ears felt as though pegs were being driven into them, and his head throbbed. The pain increased when he opened the door, but he ignored it and dropped to the ground. The two security men from the hangar were now running under the fuselage. One of them—the squad leader, apparently—slowed and drew his sidearm from its holster. He slapped a magazine into the grip of the weapon and pulled back the slide.

Jenison knew the man would be a fool to shoot at him under a fuel–laden aircraft wing with hundreds of spectators in the field of fire. Just the same, he hurried to the rear of the truck.

He removed his sneakers and climbed the ladder to the top of the fuel container. He slipped out of his jeans and briefs and kicked them to the ground. The engine volume jumped suddenly. He looked up at the cockpit and saw the pilot waving frantically, shouting despite the noise. He guessed the man had advanced the throttles in an attempt to frighten him away from the plane, perhaps thinking he was dealing with a drunken spectator. What else could he think? Jenison extended his left arm toward the cockpit and held up his thumb. More power was better. He didn't wait to see the pilot's reaction, but turned instead to face the engine.

Naked in the sun, his hair whipping around his ears and forehead, he thought briefly of Susie Greene, and was ashamed. He could not share her fate, nor would he remain to comfort her. He was escaping Flint, but he was running from Susie, too— abandoning her just as he had abandoned so many others. It could not be helped.

His burgeoning guilt vanished when the security squad leader crept into view under the wing. The man's fatigues were blackened with sweat, and his chest heaved. His hands overlapped in a vise–like grip on the butt of his M18 as he stopped and spread his feet in a combat firing stance. He shouted something and raised the gun. Jenison ignored him and concentrated on the engine.

The stiff wind generated by the suction of the main compressor fan urged him forward. He breathed deeply several times, his eyes fused on the howling engine thirty feet away. He clenched and unclenched his fists then sprang up on his toes and began to run. The rush of intake air amplified his natural speed so that by the time he had traversed half the length of the fuel container he felt like an Olympic sprinter. He laughed.

Ten feet from the engine, Jenison dove toward the hot black blur of the compressor fan.

☐

"Who are you today, old woman?" Jenison looked up from his suitcase to the stout figure in the bedroom doorway. "Clan Mother or demon?"

Susie Greene threw back her head and laughed. The gesture was masculine, not at all like the Tuscarora Clan Mother. "I am Hino, of course."

"You are a liar, Flint." Even after three hundred years Jenison still wasn't sure who or what the demon was. In recent decades he had toyed with the possibility that the being was a stranded alien, but his powers were so great, so apparently magical, that it was convenient to think of him as Flint, the demon once feared by his tribe. The Onguiaarhas had known the demon as Tawiskaro or Hanis'he'ono, though most called him Flint, after the hard stone of which his heart was made. But the Onguiaarhas had vanished long ago. Almost nothing remained of them except "Niagara," the European corruption of their name. Niagara and Jenison.

Flint entered the tiny room and stepped to the window. He rubbed a circle of frost from the glass with Susie's calloused fingers. The wind hooted as it blasted a steady snowfall around the mobile home and sent tremors through the walls and floor. "This is not a day for you, *Deoneyont*."

Jenison scowled at the sound of the Seneca word. It meant "red hot." The demon had given him the nickname after he'd tried to kill himself with fire. Flint turned from the window and sat on the edge of the bed. Jenison resumed packing his suitcase.

"Was it a good death this time, Deoneyont?"

"Yes," Jenison answered without hesitation. Of all his deaths since the summer of 1680, several stood out as especially bad. The fire, the French bayonets, and the anthill would not soon be forgotten. Still, there had been a few easy ones. He remembered his decapitation almost fondly: the guillotine had been as painless as advertised. But even the easy deaths weren't good, for they didn't last. The demon was always there to patch him together again, to repair and revive him after a brief taste of oblivion.

"What was it like, Deoneyont?"

"You don't know?"

"1 cannot read thoughts."

Jenison jammed the last of his belongings into the suitcase and zipped the cover shut. He stood in front of the dressing table mirror and saw the reflection of an olive–skinned young man with short black hair. The one hundred eighty year–old guillotine scar was gone—his fingers and thumb crept gently over his throat to confirm it. All of his scars were gone: the bullet holes, the saber wounds, the burns. Flint had always made sure there were scars—mementos of his failures—but this time Jenison had been resurrected without a blemish. This was not a reassembly, not a patch job. This body was *new*.

The jet turbine blades had left no more than bone slivers and scorched bits of meat—of that he was sure. There could not have been much for the demon to work with, yet here he was. Whatever had remained of him Flint had somehow scraped up from the tarmac and transported two miles to the Tuscarora Reservation. Jenison wondered what that might have looked like, and could imagine only B movie special effects. A well–done hamburger man plodding through the cornfields to Susie

Greene's home—bits of seared flesh squirming like worms along the tarmac, congealing into a mass the size of a beach ball. Expelling aviation fuel and tar. Coughing out greasy lumps of gravel as it rolled home.

How was it possible? Had Flint rebuilt Jenison's ruined form by some genetic process? If so, how then did his memories remain intact? Was it magic or science?

"It was nothing," Jenison said finally. "A flash of light followed by blackness, then nothing." He slipped into a flannel shirt and buttoned it, tucking the tail into his jeans. "I woke up here with Susie forcing me to drink herb tea." He nodded slowly. "It was a good death."

"*I* enjoyed it," Flint said. "It was a spectacular demise. Very messy."

Jenison snorted and put on his parka. He hefted the suitcase and walked to the door.

"Where will you go?"

"To find the One Way, demon." Jenison looked over his shoulder. "Will you tell me where to look?"

"You always ask me that." Flint lifted his old woman arms and shrugged. "There is only one way to end this, but you must find it for yourself, Deoneyont. Do you grow weary of the bargain?"

"Yes. You knew that three hundred years ago"

"I suppose I did."

"You won't tell me then?"

"Even between friends there must be secrets." Flint sniggered. "I will tell you only that you are getting warmer, Deoneyont."

"This is not justice, demon."

"You did not come to me for justice, fool. You came to me for murder."

"I came to you to avenge Awenhai."

"You were delighted to accept my terms."

True enough, Jenison thought. He had greedily embraced Flint's offer of everlasting life.

□

The Matriarch Gadjiqsa sat with the four Onguiaarha Clan Mothers on the dais at the rear of the meeting house. She signaled to the Doorkeepers as the last of the adult villagers took their places in the crowded room. The guards nodded their garish wooden masks and sealed the entrance with birch bark panels.

Gadjiqsa's false face pivoted slowly as she surveyed the assembled tribe. Orange light from the wall torches flickered over the corn husk mask and her doeskin robe. "The fair and kindly Awenhai shall be mourned," she said in a strong clear voice, "but we will not send our warriors against the French muskets—that would be suicide."

The older people seated in front sighed with relief, but a murmur of discontent and shouts of dismay rose from the young men crowding the rear of the longhouse.

"No!" a warrior named Kienuka shouted. The room fell silent as he strode to the dais of the Clan Mothers and stood before Gadjiqsa. "If the French decide to kill all of us, one at a time, will we do more than grieve?" His voice was calm, but his rage hung in the air like a cold mist. "Is that how it is to be, old woman?"

Kienuka was to have married Awenhai, but she was murdered a month before the wedding day. A hunting party discovered her mutilated corpse near Cayuga Creek. Two French uniform buttons and an empty wine jug found at the scene left no doubt as to what had happened.

The Onguiaarhas petitioned the commander at Fort Conti for the trial of the three soldiers seen in the area at the time Awenhai was found, but to no avail: French justice required more evidence than a bottle and some buttons. Had the tribe been larger, they would have made war on the French, laying siege to the small garrison at the mouth of the river, but the predations of Seneca raiders over the years had weakened the tribe. The Onguiaarhas would do nothing.

"There will be no war, Kienuka, and there will be no reprisals," Gadjiqsa said. The Clan Mothers solemnly nodded their affirmation of the decree. Gadjiqsa was Matriarch, and her word was law.

"They murdered my bride, and you say I must do nothing?"

"We will not sacrifice the tribe to avenge one girl," the old woman said, "and you will not bring destruction upon us." Her voice was as hard as stone.

"Where, then, is justice to be found? How am I to avenge her?"

"Pray to Hino," Gadjiqsa replied. "He detests evil creatures. Hino will settle with these French."

The Onguiaarhas believed that the benevolent thunder god Hino lived in a crystal cave behind the great crescent waterfall at the neck of the river. Kienuka had always taken part in Hino's festivals and ceremonies, but he had never thought of himself as religious, and he had never really worshipped the thunder god.

"I will not pray to Hino," he said. "I shall *go* to him! If he will not avenge Awenhai, then I will." Kienuka glared at the Matriarch, expecting censure, but she said nothing. He turned his back on her and stormed out of the longhouse.

The next morning he went alone to the river. He used wooden stakes and ropes of deer sinew to cross the deadly north rapids to Thagonhsowes, the cliff island that split the river into two mighty cataracts. There he climbed down the rock face separating the falls, into the deep gorge that had once been home to the stone giants.

Hino's cave was said to lie behind the greater fall, the crescent–shaped cataract to the south. Kienuka stood among the huge black rocks that jutted like teeth from the crescent's north edge, and searched for a way to get behind the falling water. The crescent towered above him to the height of thirty or forty warriors and seemed to pour all the world's water into the gorge. About a quarter of the way up its edge, a sliver of black appeared and disappeared in the churning white water. At the level of the black sliver was a narrow ledge that led behind the fall. Kienuka climbed toward it.

The spray that fell from above and rebounded from the stones stung him like thrown pebbles. He moved slowly upward, wedging his feet and hands in the shale whenever he could. He knew what would become of him were he to slip into the column of falling water. The dismembered bodies of men and deer that had been swept over the falls were a common sight down river.

Much of the time he groped about blindly, holding his breath as surges of white water cascaded over him. When he reached the narrow ledge, the falling water and gusts of wind blowing up from the base of the cataract made it difficult to stand, let alone rest, so he kept moving. He shuffled behind the fall with his back scraping against the wall of shale. The torrent coursing over him forced him to keep his eyes closed. His left hand probed ahead as he moved, while his right cupped his nose and mouth so he could breathe without inhaling water. After what seemed an eternity, the shelf widened and he moved into a pocket of cool air. He wiped the water from his face and hair, then opened his eyes.

Kienuka found himself in a massive hollow gouged from the shale by a millennium of erosion—a cave into which sunlight was filtered to a dull green by the wall of water. He fell to his knees and brought his bruised, bleeding hands together in a gesture of supplication. "Hino!" he shouted, barely able to hear himself above the roar of the falling water, "the French have murdered Awenhai. Will you give me vengeance?"

He waited patiently for a response, but heard only the crash of water and the howling wind. Dejected, he bowed his head and sang the death chant of his people. He had scarcely begun when the wet black shale before him glistened with brilliant green light. The sodden depths of the cave glimmered like a vast emerald. "Hino?"

The booming voice that suddenly answered was not that of a man. "You ask much, *haqgeeah*."

"Please!" It took the remainder of Kienuka's strength and concentration to speak. "I will do anything!"

"You offer more than you can know, shabby little man."
The words seemed to come from the water and the shale. From everywhere and nowhere.

"I will do anything, Hino!"

The voice laughed, and it was the sound of the river breaking stone. "I shall kill these French for you, haqgeeah, but you must pay the price. You must do something for *me*."

"Anything!"

"You must live forever."

Kienuka's eyes widened. He shook his head with wonder. "Immortality? That is no price to pay. That is a greater gift than vengeance."

"It is a *price*." The voice was mirthless. "Think well before you agree. Immortality may not be to your liking."

"To be as a god would be very much to my liking. Only a fool would refuse such a gift."

"Perhaps. We will make a bargain, you and I, ragged man, and I shall tell you this: you will tire of life and wish to die."

"Never!" Kienuka laughed with joy.

"You will wish to die, and I will let you, if you can find the One Way."

"You shall be disappointed."

"Ha! Remember: there will be only one way for you to die. Your enemies shall perish while you remain young and fit. Your mind will not fail with age, yet you will yearn for death."

"Why do you offer this?" Kienuka was more curious than suspicious.

"You shall be my companion, ragged man," the voice answered, laughing. "You shall entertain me. It will amuse me much to watch you search for the One Way. Are we agreed, then?"

In his lust for eternal life, Kienuka had nearly forgotten the purpose of his quest. "You will avenge Awenhai?"

"Yes."

"Then we have a bargain, Hino." The warrior stood, his exhaustion and pain forgotten.

The laughing water echoed in the cave one last time, then merged with the roar of the cataract.

Kienuka returned to his tribe.

That winter Fort Conti was visited by cholera. Only the priests and the medical officer survived. Kienuka rejoiced at the news of the French catastrophe, and made a prayer of thanks to Hino, but his joy was short lived, for the disease then spread to the Onguiaarhas. By the Spring of 1681, only a handful of the tribe remained.

When the weather had warmed enough for corn planting, the Onguiaarhas who had not succumbed to cholera were massacred by marauding Senecas. Kienuka himself was killed—his skull crushed by an Iroquois war hammer. He returned from the peaceful oblivion of death to find himself alone. It was then that he knew it was not Hino behind the great crescent fall, but some Other, and that he had sacrificed the tribe for his immortality.

Kienuka began to think of the One Way.

☐

Kienuka, you should have died that summer. You should have gone with Awenhai. William Jenison looked into the face of Susie Greene and met the unblinking gaze of the demon. "I was a fool to bargain with you," he said aloud.

"Why do you hate me so, Deoneyont? Have I not given you a great gift?"

"It is a curse, demon—as you well know." Jenison had outlived hundreds of friends, lovers, and children. Everyone he had ever known and loved or respected was dead or would die. The dead haunted him; Awenhai still haunted him. The smallest things would remind him of them—a certain painting, the flash of familiar eyes in a crowd, a song. Not a day passed that he did not weep for them. He longed to follow the dead, to share their fate. "How do you bear the loneliness of immortality, Flint?"

"I am not lonely. I have *you*."

12

"I'll find the One Way." Jenison turned and walked into the kitchen.

"Where will you go?"

"You always ask me that," Jenison said. He opened the kitchen door and stepped down into the snow.

"I'll follow," Flint called after him. "I'll watch!"

You always do. Jenison closed the door behind him and waded through the drifting snow to the jeep. He threw his suitcase into the back seat and climbed in, then started the engine and rolled down his window to watch the snow fall into the meadow. He would miss this place. His people were gone, but he had found a home here with the kindly Tuscaroras. He tried to recall the excitement he had felt as a child when the winds blowing south from Lake Ontario met the rush of cold air moving north from Erie, filling the Onguiaarha forest with hip–deep snow. But too much time had passed: he felt only despair.

When he returned to the trailer, Flint was gone. He found Susie asleep on the living room couch, and gently shook her. "It's time," he said.

The old woman opened her eyes. She nodded and rose.

They drove into the city in silence. When they reached the bus station, Jenison looked at Susie and tried to smile, but his eyes began to water and his nose stung. Her chemotherapy had not worked, he knew, and she would be gone soon, "I'm sorry—"

"Don't be." Susie placed a finger to his lips. "I under–stand." She sniffed and began fumbling with her seat belt. "Where will you go?"

"Hawaii. There's an active volcano there. I don't think He can reconstruct me if my genetic material is destroyed. Molten lava will assure that."

Susie opened the passenger door and slipped outside. "And if he already has your genetic material?"

Jenison shrugged and stepped into the growing blizzard. "I'll find another way."

"Perhaps the One Way." The old woman smiled across the hood of the Jeep.

They walked to the station together and stopped outside the main entrance.

Jenison hugged the old woman there in front of the frost–rimed windows, squeezing her like a drowning man clutching a bit of flotsam. "Goodbye, Susie."

She hugged him back and kissed his forehead, then wriggled free and pushed him toward the door. "Goodbye, Grandfather."

William Jenison wiped his eyes with his fist and entered the building. He didn't look back.

THE NO SHOW

"Lift your right leg," Doctor Marrier said.

Stanley Kowalczyk moaned theatrically as he clutched the padded edges of the examination table and raised his leg several inches. "It hurts bad, Doc." He winced and clenched his teeth. "I can't—"

Marrier grabbed the younger man's left heel with his left hand, and with practiced strength, rapidly swung the leg to a vertical position. Kowalczyk was too surprised to feign discomfort without a pause to collect himself. He cocked his head and stared at his leg in shock. "Ouch," he said finally, scowling at his extremity as if it had somehow betrayed him.

Marrier turned on the small dictation recorder in his free hand. *"This twenty–eight–year–old white male alleges disability due to a 'bad back',"* he said in a brusque voice. *"He is seventy–three inches tall and weighs one hundred ninety–two pounds. Blood pressure is 128 over 75, pulse 80, respiration 20. He is of medium build and appears his stated age. He entered the examination room with a marked left limp and guarding posture; however, I observed his approach to the office through the parking lot: his gait at that time was normal and his posture was good. He disrobed for this examination with remarkable agility. He is able to tandem walk and heel/toe walk with some*

15

encouragement. Range of motion of the lumbosacral spine is full, with subjective pain. There is no spasm or obvious deformity. Straight leg raising is negative." He released Kowalczyk's heel and watched the leg drop to the examination table with a thud.

Marrier continued his examination, dictating as he went. His hands probed the abdomen. He checked reflexes and cranial nerves. He listened for abnormal breath sounds and pockets of fluid. There was nothing out of the ordinary. Heart, lungs, liver, extremities, skin—all seemed normal. Except for the track marks. The arms and legs were patterned with scores of tiny punctures in various stages of healing. But this was consistent with the history of intravenous drug use. There was no evidence of the opportunistic infections typical of AIDS, which was good. He switched off the recorder and smiled.

"Sit up please, son, and open your mouth."

Kowalczyk rolled to an upright position, his legs dangling over the edge of the table.

Marrier clicked the recorder back on and clasped Kowalczyk's lower jaw with his ancient hand. He squeezed with such force that the younger man's eyes bulged. *"The claimant is partially edentulous, with extensive caries."* He thumbed the recorder's pause switch and said, "Son, you really should have taken better care of your teeth. I'm afraid it's too late now."

"Unnohhh," Stanley agreed, nodding weakly in Marrier's powerful grip.

At eighty–seven, Doctor Marrier still had the strong fingers of a handball enthusiast. He played three evenings a week and could still trounce men of sixty. While much of his physical endurance and agility had progressively deteriorated after he had turned fifty, he had lost nothing mentally: he was still a superb diagnostician. In sixty years of practice in internal medicine he had seen just about everything. What he saw before him now was a wasted life: a young man who had frittered away his youth, succumbing to peer pressure at the expense of his education and his integrity.

He released Kowalczyk's jaw. "You can put your pants on now, son. Leave your shirt off."

Kowalczyk slid from the examination table slowly, using his arms for support. He gasped and grimaced as though in agony. "When do I get my checks, Doc?"

"Checks?" Marrier asked, smiling. "Oh, you mean money." He removed the stethoscope from his neck and tucked it in his lab coat pocket. "I'm afraid that's not up to me. I provide reports of my examination findings to the state agency and *they* decide whether or not someone is disabled."

"But I can't work. My back hurts bad all the time." Kowalczyk arched his spine and rubbed both hands on the small of his back by way of emphasis.

"Of course," Marrier agreed, nodding, his wrinkled pink face creased with a knowing smile. "I have something here for pain—something that will make you feel much better."

Kowalczyk brightened at the unanticipated prospect of obtaining painkillers. He grinned slyly, his eyes squinted with curiosity. What drug did this old man have in mind to ease his pain? Demerol? Oxycontin? If it was something he didn't want for himself, he could easily sell it on the street to get the money for something he needed. His mouth watered.

"Just let me finish my dictation," Marrier said as he rolled a wheelchair toward Kowalczyk. "Have a seat, won't you? I'll finish up and then we'll talk about what's wrong with you."

Kowalczyk slipped into his soiled jeans and sat down in the wheelchair. He put on his sweat socks and engineer boots as the doctor switched on the recorder and completed his report.

"In conclusion. this claimant has subjective back pain with no clinical evidence of disk herniation, nerve root compression, or scoliosis. X–rays of the lumbosacral spine taken ..." Marrier paused, flipping through Kowalczyk's chart for the radiologist's report. *". . . three months ago show no abnormalities. Despite the history of polysubstance abuse stared earlier, review of systems is negative. Provisional diagnosis is malingering."* He switched the machine off.

"What's this 'maringling', Doc? Is *that* my problem?"
Kowalczyk leaned forward in the wheelchair, hands clasped and
elbows resting on the arm supports.

"*Malingering*. It's a big problem for all of us. It's the cause
of your pain."

"Yeah, it does hurt real bad, Doc. All the time. Can you
give me something for it?" Kowalczyk licked his lips.

Doctor Marrier rose and stepped behind the wheelchair. He
massaged the young man's shoulders briefly, then pinched his
cheek amiably. He laughed quietly, somehow amused by this
young devil's long, oily hair and macabre tattoos. There was
something genuinely funny about the large picture on his right
upper arm: an expertly illustrated vulture perched on a bone
above an unfurled scroll bearing the legend "Mother."

"Of course, son. We'll take care of that pain right now.
You're not afraid of needles, are you?"

Kowalczyk choked off a laugh.

"Of course not!" Marrier chuckled, slipping a syringe from
his pocket. He removed a medium gauge needle from its sterile
wrapper and screwed it on the barrel of the syringe. "Now, son,
I want you to look straight ahead. I'm going to remove a small
amount of fluid from your spine to determine just what drugs
will best help you. It may hurt a bit, but it won't last long." The
lie left an unpleasant taste in his mouth as it always did, but that
could not be helped. "Ready?"

"Just fix my pain, Doc."

Working quietly behind Kowalczyk's back, Marrier
removed the safety sheath from the needle and uncapped a tiny
vial of transparent fluid. He punctured the rubber seal with the
needle and inverted the vial, drawing back the plunger of the
syringe with his thumb. He flicked the syringe briskly several
times and depressed the plunger until a jet of clear liquid darted
from the needle tip. Satisfied that no air remained in the
chamber, he pushed Kowalczyk forward in his wheelchair and
swabbed the base of his skull with an alcohol sponge.

"Okay, now touch your chin to your chest and hold it there.
This will pinch a little." Marrier deftly pierced the tissue

between the skull and first cervical vertebra with the needle and drew back again on the plunger. The clear fluid return confirmed that he had properly tapped the cisterna magna. He slowly injected the contents of the syringe. When he had finished, he bent the needle and dumped the syringe into a red biohazard control box.

"What you gonna give me, Doc?" Kowalczyk asked eagerly.

"I've already given you something to relax you, son. You can sit up now," Marrier said jovially as he spun the young man around in his chair.

"I thought you was gonna test some of my fluid."

"I lied." Marrier crossed his arms and looked down at Kowalczyk over the lenses of his steel–rimmed glasses. "Lift your left leg, please, son."

Stanley Kowalczyk's bewildered expression quickly changed to one of alarm. "My leg won't move!" he cried.

"Isn't that better? No more pain, right?" Marrier grinned broadly and scratched his bald spot, running his fingers through the shock of curly white hair encircling his head.

Wide–eyed with growing terror, Kowalczyk struggled against the effects of the drug, but he was paralyzed from the neck down. He tried to move his arms without success. He couldn't even writhe. He could taste the bitter fear on his tongue. He could breathe, see, speak, and hear—but no more. It was as though he were encased in wax. "What'd you do to me, you dirty old mother—"

"Ha!" Marrier interrupted, beaming. "Is that the thanks I get for helping you out of your misery? You will never feel pain again, and you repay me with insults? Oh, you'll undergo some emotional distress for a short while, but nothing quite as bad as what you've put others through."

Kowalczyk breathed more and more rapidly, nearly hyperventilating. The expression on his face alternated between one of fear and hate. "You gonna kill me, man?"

"Some people might call it that," Marrier answered. "I prefer to think of it as making you a more productive citizen."

The perspiration beaded on Kowalczyk's face broke into rivulets that streamed down his neck and shoulders. His chest heaved.

"I've gone over your records very carefully. The questionnaires you completed for the disability examiner were most helpful, as were the discharge summaries and clinic notes from the county medical center. You are not a very nice man at all, son. You won't be missed." Marrier paged through Kowalczyk's background material.

"You're a welfare recipient. You have never held a job and clearly have no intention of ever being a useful member of society. You freely admit to drinking yourself into a stupor whenever you can. You have a two hundred dollar a day drug habit. You acknowledge stealing—"

"I have to boost shit to get what I need!"

"Of course. You 'boost' the property of others to support your sordid habits, because a welfare entitlement check just isn't enough. In the past ten years you have had more than a dozen hospitalizations for detoxification that cost the taxpayers fifteen thousand dollars each, on average.

"Son, you are a menace to yourself and society at large. You are parasite, a sociopath. I'd love to see your criminal record, but I've a fair enough idea of what it contains. I just wonder how many little old ladies you've mugged, how many homes you've burglarized, how much hurt and mayhem you've wrought."

"I don't gotta listen to this preacher shit, mother—"

"Tsk! Tsk! There is no need for profanity." Marrier pouted and wagged his head slowly. "Young man, you are what my nephew George used to call 'a waste of skin.' Well, we're going to change that now. I'm going to help you make a contribution to your fellow man. I will do a service for society by implementing your ... *removal*. You will render a service by making a rather substantive gift"

Kowalczyk was weeping now. Strands of mucous oozed from his nose, and his cheeks were wet with tears. "I just came

20

here 'cause my caseworker told me to file a claim," he sobbed. "I didn't do nothin' wrong, man. I don't wanna die!"

"Come now, Mr. Kowalczyk," Marrier said encouragingly as he patted Kowalczyk's head. "Chin up! You're not going to die—at least not completely. I'm going to make you sleep. 'To sleep, perchance to dream', as the poet said. In two days the organ harvesters will come to collect you. I wanted to tell you, by the way, how pleased I was to find that you hadn't damaged your vital organs and that your last HIV test was negative. Oh, your life will continue in a very real sense. You'll be spread a bit thin, though," he chuckled in his peculiar fashion and turned Kowalczyk's chair around. He pushed the wheelchair toward the examination room door.

"Your heart will turn up somewhere, identified as that of an accident victim. It will be transplanted into the body of a deserving recipient. Your lungs, marrow, liver, kidneys, and corneas will be given to the needy as well. You will live a long and fruitful life, although you will be blissfully unaware of it. Unfortunately for you, your consciousness will come to an end. Medical science has not yet achieved the surgical sophistication needed to transplant a human brain, let alone its contents. Someday, perhaps. Though I don't know what use might be made of a mind such as yours."

"Please don't kill me, man," Kowalczyk blubbered. "I'll be good. I'll be good!"

"It's too late for promises, Mr. Kowalczyk," Marrier observed as he rolled his victim out of the room. He turned down the carpeted hallway and stopped before his storeroom door. He dug in his pants pocket for the key. "You are about to become a productive citizen. Now hush!"

Marrier unlocked the door and swung it inward. He sampled the air with a cautious sniff. "My goodness!" he cooed, as if addressing a baby. "Somebody made pooh–pooh!"

Kowalczyk gasped, partly from the stench that enveloped him, partly from the sight that met his eyes when Marrier flipped the light switch.

Four young men strapped in wheelchairs lined the wall opposite the door. They wore only diapers, and each was connected by plastic tubing to intravenous feeding bags. All four had identically sutured incisions on their foreheads. Each man stared vacantly and drooled. Kowalczyk groaned when he saw that there was room for one more wheelchair. "Oh, God! What's wrong with them? What'd you do to them?"

"I've improved them." Marrier patted Kowalczyk's oily head again. "They will finally lead productive lives! When the organ harvesting people come they will have five donors: three black men, one yellow man, and one white man. You." Marrier gestured to the heavy brown youth in the first chair. Can you believe that Mr. Jones over there accused me of racism? Good Lord! This is about as close to the Brotherhood of Man as any of you will ever get." He turned the chair around and backed it into the remaining spot against the wall.

"Lemme go, man!" Kowalczyk wailed. "I'll be good! I'll be good!"

"Yes, you will, son. You certainly will," Marrier agreed as he headed for the door. "Excuse me, but I've got a thing or two to do before business hours come to an end. I'll be back to take care of you shortly. I don't have a friend at the electric company," he added cheerfully, as he switched off the light and closed the door. Kowalczyk's frantic screams were muffled by the heavy oak door panels.

Marrier returned to his office and sat in his leather wing chair. He took a moment to light a cigar, then picked up the telephone handset and rapidly punched a familiar number. "Hello?" he said after a moment, exhaling a cloud of thick smoke. "Disability? This is Doctor Morris Marrier. I'd like to speak with the Scheduling Unit, please."

He tapped his cigar over the crystal ashtray his wife had given him as a birthday present five years before her death at the hands of a street thug. Gladys had been a loving wife and a great receptionist. He missed her tremendously.

"Hello? Doctor Marrier here," he said, swiveling in his chair as the receiver crackled. "I'm calling with regard to Mr.

Stanley Kowalczyk. He was scheduled for an examination at four o'clock this afternoon. I'm afraid he didn't show." He smiled contentedly and puffed his cigar.

"My time is valuable, Miss. This is the fifth no–show this month. I simply can't afford this—time is money, you know. Will you speak to your Medical Relations Office about compensation? I'd hate to have to withdraw my services over something as silly as this. You'll ask them to arrange payment then? Good. That is satisfactory."

Marrier leaned forward and consulted his date book. "There is another matter. I have here a work order for an examination on one Angel Rivera. I'd like to schedule an appointment for him. Of course I'll hold. Thank you."

Morris Marrier, M.D., reclined in his chair and tapped his cigar over the crystal ashtray.

He wondered if Gladys would approve.

VERLIER'S WILL

Unlike the other nurses, Judith checked Verlier's urinary catheter every hour. Every two hours she put drops in his eyes, repositioned him, and cleaned his mouth, carefully suctioning the accumulated mucous. Twice each shift she checked his rectal catheter and collection bag. She bathed him like a baby, scrubbing him thoroughly but gently over his entire body. She swabbed his nostrils clean and exercised his limbs.

"You're stronger today, Tommy," she always said. "Nobody thinks you'll get better, but they're all wrong."

Since Verlier regained consciousness he had recovered the use of his eyes. It took tremendous concentration but he could now shift his gaze from the window to the wall clock in five minutes. He could alter his labored breathing, even move his tongue slightly if he worked at it long enough. Soon he'd be able to move his arms and legs.

Getting better, he thought. Soon they'll remove the feeding tube and I'll sit up. In six months I'll be walking. Christ, I'm lucky.

Verlier still wasn't sure what had happened. He knew he had been in a car wreck and suffered brain trauma but couldn't remember any of it. He figured it had happened five months ago, but he wasn't sure. Sometimes he slipped into the nightmarish twilight of semi–consciousness and lost track of time. No one ever mentioned the date, but he could watch the clock and count shift changes. He could see the sky through the blinds. A score of patients had occupied the other bed since he woke. Five months sounded about right. And each day he grew stronger, each day he regained more control.

Judith gave Verlier his will to live, and each day he loved her more. When he left the hospital, he planned to divorce Karin and woo the woman who had nursed him back from oblivion. He'd live a better life—a life without nightly arguments, a life with no booze or concern for upward mobility. Maybe there would even be kids.

Just at shift change one afternoon, Verlier watched through the bed rails as Judith entered the room. Doctor Feigling was with her. Something was wrong.

"Hi, Tommy." Judith stood at the foot of the bed and dabbed wadded tissue at her eyes.

Hi, Beautiful.

"They'll be here any moment, Judy," Feigling said. Almost as he spoke, Karin entered the room with a tall, gaunt man in a three–piece suit.

Verlier shifted his eyes to get a better view of his guests. Karin hadn't visited once in months. Now she was here with what? A divorce lawyer?

"Judy," Feigling said, "this is Karin Verlier and Tod Toadsfall, the hospital's Ombudsman."

"My pleasure." Toadsfall extended a hand. After a moment his hand returned unshaken to his side.

"Let's finish this." Karin said softly.

"Doctor, this man is recovering," Judith said. "He has plantar reflexes, improved muscle tone, and EEG patterns well beyond epileptiform spikes. His breathing—"

"I know," Feigling said. "You've done well."

Toadsfall smiled. "But his living will is indisputable. He does not wish to exist like this."

No, Verlier thought. My God.

Judith turned to Karin. "What if Tommy changed his mind? If they remove his feeding tube he'll die of dehydration. That might take three, maybe five days. Imagine the agony of it. What if he wants to live?"

"Ms. Weston." Toadsfall's voice was pure scorn. "Even if he were cognizant of his circumstances, there is nothing to suggest he'd think differently. There *is* plenty to suggest that he's oblivious. Besides, we've dehydrated patients functioning at much higher levels, including a woman who was able to *ask* for food."

"I'll go to the Health Department. They'll investigate."

Toadsfall frowned. "I'd suggest you do nothing to jeopardize your position. Doctor?"

Feigling drew back the sheet.

Verlier felt a sting on his belly then a slithering sensation in his guts. Feigling stepped away with a handful of slick tubing.

"Done," Toadsfall said, and escorted Karin from the room.

Feigling shook his head and followed them.

No, Verlier thought. His stomach was a bubbling cauldron of fear.

"Tommy?"

Verlier looked slowly at Judith. She held a syringe up where he could see it.

"This will make it easier. Painless."

But I'm getting better.

"No one will suspect—they *want* you dead."

I love you.

"Tell me it's okay, Tommy—that you forgive me." Tears welled in Judith's eyes.

Verlier tried not to think of the future that would not be. Instead, he mustered his waning strength.

He blinked.

VOODOO, VOUDOUN

Jake Fifo stepped from the elevator and groped for the keys through the hole in his jacket pocket. The key ring had migrated through the lining almost to the middle of his back. He twisted himself like a hunchback, wriggling his arm up to the elbow in bunched fabric. Finally he snagged the keys. "I've been a millionaire for three weeks now, damn it," he said. "Tonight I'm buying a new goddamned wardrobe—and the Vendetta 210."

"Pardon me?"

Jake looked up and saw a short man standing near his office door. "Sorry," Jake said. "Just thinking out loud. Are you here to see me?"

"Are you Jacob Fiffo?"

"Fifo." Jake opened the door and inspected his visitor. The man was dark–skinned, about sixty. He wore a blue pinstripe suit and brown wing tips. Gray eyes. Broad nose. A smile jammed with perfect white teeth. Surely someone annoying. "What do you want?" Jake asked brusquely.

"Good morning, Mr. Fifo," the old man said, extending a hand perfectly fitted in a black kid glove.

Jake reluctantly shook the proffered hand. "Who are you?"

"Leon DuBois of the HSA." He flipped open a billfold.

Jake caught a glimpse of a photo I.D. and badge before DuBois tucked the billfold back into his coat. "You don't look like a government agent."

DuBois shrugged. "I have just a few questions. You'll be finished in no time."

Jake turned on the lights and waved his visitor in. He closed the door and pulled a chair to the front of his desk. "Have a seat."

He removed a stack of envelopes and two small packages from his mailbox. He tossed the parcels into a bin near the door and placed the envelopes in a basket on his desk. He sat facing DuBois and turned on the desktop computer. The machine whined like a tiny jet warming for takeoff.

DuBois sat quietly.

Jake's thoughts wandered back to the Vendetta 210. He could easily afford the purchase of the car. He had been daydreaming about it since breakfast. He couldn't wait to see the expression on the salesman's face when he handed him a hundred and forty grand in cash. The more he thought about it, the more restless he became. But DuBois showed no sign of going anywhere.

Jake cleared his throat. "Nuts?" He slid a bowl of pista–chios toward DuBois.

The old man shook his head.

Jake pried a nut open and popped the meat into his mouth. He tossed the shells at an overflowing cup and missed. He swallowed and raised an eyebrow. "Time is money."

DuBois grinned and unbuckled his valise, opening it just wide enough to admit his hand. The bag croaked softly.

Jake strained to look inside. "You got a frog in there?"

"No." DuBois hastily withdrew a black notebook and snapped the valise shut. He shoved the valise out of view and began to flip pages with a gloved thumb. "My superiors are concerned that your business is in conflict with certain . . . laws. Your advertisement—"

Jake grunted. "I've been through this with the Postal Inspectors and the IRS." He slid a sheet of paper across the desk. "Here's my ad. It's completely legal."

DuBois took the sheet and began to read aloud. "'VOODOO MIRACLE! The Ancient Craft of Voodoo and the Oriental Science of Acupuncture JOIN FORCES to make you feel years younger! Throw away those crutches! Sleep peacefully! No more rheumatism! Sometimes Works — Sometimes Not. BELIEF IS THE MAIN INGREDIENT! Based in Folklore. We Make No Claims.'" He shook his head and tapped the endorsement at the bottom of the handbill. "Who is Dolores Eames? 'I feel twenty years younger!' she says. 'My arthritis no longer pains me, thanks to the Voodoo Miracle!'" DuBois shot Jake a stern look. "It's unlawful to use false endorsements."

Jake whirled in his chair and flicked his index finger sharply against a framed document hanging on the wall. "This is Mrs. Eames' unsolicited letter of endorsement. I've had several dozen like it in the past ten months."

"Just how do you earn such glowing praise?"

"For a hundred bucks I perform a Voodoo ritual with the traditional doll, silver pins, and incense. I use the acupuncture techniques outlined on the wall chart behind you. I do exactly what our ad promises: no more, no less."

"Mail order Voodoo acupuncture?" DuBois looked over his shoulder at the anatomical diagrams. The reflex points for needle punctures to treat various ailments were indicated by red stars. Black lines connected the stars to procedure names and numbers.

"Would you like to see?"

"Please." DuBois flipped to a blank page in his book and took out a ball–point pen.

Jake cleared away the clutter on his desk: plastic dolls, boxes of pins, correspondence, red pistachio shells, letter opener, staple remover, tape, disposable rubber gloves. He plowed the stuff into two piles with his arms. Nutshells and dolls clattered to the floor.

He donned a pair of gloves and took an envelope from his "IN" basket. "My clients send hair samples," he explained. "I don't touch them. Sometimes they send other things." He pointed to the parcel bin and shivered. "I used to open those, but people send crazy stuff: urine, feces, dentures. One package had a finger in it. Now I return them all unopened." He ran the envelope through the letter opener and removed a brief note in cramped blue cursive, a personal check, and a hank of red hair. Jake's hands settled on the computer keyboard and an input screen came up. He entered some information from the letter and stored it. The computer warbled and a "READY" message appeared on the monitor. He placed the check in the middle desk drawer.

"Okay." He cracked his knuckles. "This is Yolanda Giles of Meridian, Mississippi, a thirty–one year old white woman who has an 'irregular period' and 'back trouble'."

"What if she had lung cancer?"

"I'd return her money and advise her to seek proper medical care. I refuse to get sued by the family of a superstitious bumpkin who thought Voodoo Miracle could take the place of chemotherapy. I'm not losing my money to attorneys or survivors of people too dumb to see a doctor. Ten months ago I had nothing. I've built a five thousand dollar per day operation; I'm not going to hand it over to shysters." Jake smiled. "Fortunately, Yolanda's complaints are the acu–puncturist's meat and potatoes. I have an advantage over the needle men, though. Traditional Voodoo methods let me use the oriental techniques at a safe distance. I make no claims, and don't physically touch anyone, so I don't get sued for malpractice."

DuBois scribbled in his book.

Jake grabbed a pink vacuum–formed plastic doll about six inches tall. "By adding a goose feather, a length of white thread, and a lock of the client's hair" —he used thread from a spool to attach the feather to the doll's body and tied Yolanda's red hair around the doll's neck— "we have a Voodoo doll."

Jake scanned the wall chart for the appropriate reflex points and plucked two silver pins from the desk. "These have been boiled in a mixture of five finger grass, lodestone powder, Zum–Zum Koochie–Koochie Oil, cayenne pepper, and well water. One goes in at the Chungkung point—for back pain." He drove a pin home just to the left of the doll's spine. He turned the figure over. "The female trouble is covered by . . . "His eyes moved again to the chart, then he pushed the second pin into the doll's left hip. ". . . Chenching, point 24." He returned "Yolanda" to the desktop. "Now all that remains is the incantation."

"Don't you need a priest for that?"

"I'm an ordained Mambo," Jake replied. "Courtesy of the New Orleans Correspondence School." He touched the keyboard and the computer began to play "St. James Infirmary." The music quickly faded to the twangy voice of a speech synthesizer:

Erzulie, mend this woman!
Heal Yolanda Giles!
Guide her through the Abyss and back to the living,
Ease her pain, Agwe Arroyo!
Protect this earth child! Care for your little one!
Exu, Exu! Guide her gladly
From the Abyss, back through the Crossroads!

DuBois coughed softly into his hand.

"There," Jake said. "I do exactly what my ad says. Amazingly, it seems to work for some people. Mrs. Eames, for instance."

"People pay one hundred dollars for this?"

"Yep." Jake dropped his gloves into the wastebasket and sat back in his chair. "I'm averaging over five thousand bucks a day," he confided with a broad grin. "It's a gold mine!"

"It may be a gold mine, Mr. Fiffo—"

"Fifo."

"Fifo. It may be a gold mine, but it is not Voodoo."

"Not Voodoo?" Jake cocked his head. "What do you mean?"

"This mumbo–jumbo you perform is not Voodoo. In fact, there is no 'Voodoo' as you call it. The ancestral faith of the Dahomey people is Voudoun. Voudoun healing rituals use no dolls." DuBois pointed at the stack of unopened mail. "This abomination you are foisting upon these innocents is not Voudoun. It is a corrupt blend of Nineteenth Century folklore and Brazilian fetishism. 'Hoodoo' is a better description of your hoodwinking operation!"

"No Voodoo dolls? Hold on." Jake yanked a book from the credenza behind him and tossed it on the desk, knocking "Yolanda" aside in a shower of nutshells. He tapped the book vigorously with his finger. *Professor Clemenceau's Lucky Dream Book and Voodoo Primer.* "The dolls are right in here! I've followed the procedures to the letter. I've even ordered authentic materials from Mojo Man Voodoo Supplies of Shreveport."

"Professor Clemenceau was the pen name of Gladys Sterling," DuBois said. "Sterling was a Bronx flapper who made a small fortune peddling myths exploiting the 'mystical/magical legacy' of naive urban blacks. Hollywood's portrayal of Voudoun has been largely based on her books. None of them has any basis in fact; there are no Voudoun dolls."

"No Voodoo dolls?" Jake pounded the book with his fist. "That's crazy." He pointed at the door to his right and shouted, "There are twenty–five hundred of them in my washroom!"

"It is not Voudoun," DuBois repeated.

"Vood–oo, Vood–oon, so long as I get my money without going to the slammer, what difference does it make?"

DuBois looked at the ceiling and sighed.

"Anyway, why would a government agency care whether or not my business is accurate in all the details?" Jake asked, suddenly suspicious.

"I am not from a government agency."

"You showed me your ID card," Jake sputtered. "You said you were from HSA!"

"HSA is not a government agency. You assumed that." DuBois pulled out his billfold and removed the identification card. "Here, read it this time."

"Then who the Hell are you?" Jake snarled. "What's HSA?" He took the card and glanced at the old man to confirm that his face matched the photograph. What he had earlier thought to be a badge was actually a badge–shaped spiral of fine text. In order to read the tiny lettering, he had to rotate the card continuously, following the spiral from the outer edge of the badge toward the center, where it ended in a tiny cross that looked rather like an elaborate weather vane. "'Monsieur Napoleon DuBois, Houngan – 16B. Rue de Carrefour – Port Au Prince – Haiti,'" he quoted as he turned the card. He finished the rest in silence and placed the card on the desk. "You're from the Houngan Society of the Americas?"

"I am a Houngan," DuBois confirmed. He opened his valise and removed a softball–sized object wrapped in white muslin. A loud squawk came from the open case. "Hush!" he said, and placed the Thing on the desk next to "Yolanda". He rolled the fabric down, exposing a red clay pot.

Jake tried to lean forward to see the bag, but stopped short as if he had strained a back muscle. He gasped and looked at DuBois.

The old man smiled genially.

"What's a Houngan?" Jake's tongue felt thick and sluggish in his mouth. His hands tingled. He examined them with an effort. His fingers were coated with a chalky black film. Instinctively he rolled them across his thumbs, spreading the black stuff over his palms. He began to breathe in short, hungry pants.

"There's no precise English equivalent," DuBois said. He pulled another clay pot from the valise, this one wrapped in white silk. Larger than the first and less austere, it had a white glaze and a glossy blue lid. "I'm a priest and doctor rolled into one—a shaman, if you will." He placed the larger container next to the first and plunged his hands into the valise, grappling briefly with something that screeched and clucked. At length he hefted a large, struggling rooster and released it on the desktop. The creature strutted to the pistachio bowl and pecked furiously at the nuts.

Jake blinked defensively as the bird scattered pistachios in its frenzied hunt for unshelled meats. "A p–priest," he stammered, "of what ch–church?" His eyes shifted from his black–smudged hands to the rooster and back again.

"Voudoun, naturally!" DuBois's voice bore a trace of French accent that had not been there before.

"Wa ha yo don t'me?" Jake had difficulty getting the syllables past his uncooperative lips. His skin itched as though thousands of tiny ants were crawling on him. The ants were very small, but growing larger and more active with each moment. He tried to move his arms to scratch them, but his limbs only settled slowly to the desk. He was paralyzed.

"A novelty shop trick," DuBois answered breezily. He removed his suit coat and replaced it with a white blazer he had extracted from the valise.

Jake wondered what else the old man had in the bag.

"You should have kept your gloves on," DuBois said amiably. "The back of the card is coated with Retiré Bon Ange, a poison derived from the sea toad."

Jake gurgled.

"Do not be afraid," DuBois cooed. He seized the rooster by the neck. The bird squawked and flapped its wings, showering Jake with white feathers. "The poison will not kill you. It will merely make you more . . . receptive. The tetrodotoxin has disrupted your central nervous system. You will see and hear, but will be unable to do anything. By the time the effects of the poison wear off, however, you will no longer care to do anything."

DuBois gently pushed Jake back into his chair. "You are a Houngan Macoute," he continued in an unmistakable Creole accent, "a charlatan, a false prophet. We will not permit you to continue this 'Voodoo Miracle,' *blanc*." He drew himself up to his full height, such as it was. "You, my petit malfacteur, are out of business. You are working for us now."

Jake struggled to stand, to flee. It was useless; he could barely muster a cringe.

DuBois plucked four feathers from the bird and arranged them in a cross on Clemenceau's Primer. "We shall have your *gros–bon–ange*—your soul. It will go here, into the pot–de–têtê," he explained, patting the red clay pot. "The loa will come from the Govi,"—he fondled the white pot reverently— "and go here." He pressed two fingers against Jake's left temple. As if on cue, the Govi lid lifted slightly.

"Dans le têtê!" a tiny voice squeaked from within. "Dans le têtê!"

The lid clicked shut.

DuBois laughed. "He is a powerful loa. He will mount your soul and ride it like a horse. Your blasphemy will be erased; you will do his bidding for the good of Voudoun."

Jake felt a tear roll down his cheek.

"Guiné!" DuBois suddenly shouted. He thrust the rooster's head into his mouth and bit down, thrashing his own head fiercely. A spurt of blood drooled down his chin onto his white shirt as the head came free. He spat it violently across the room; it landed with a wet plop in the bin of unopened parcels.

The decapitated rooster struggled wildly.

DuBois drew a gourd rattle from his coat pocket and shook it in a brisk, steady rhythm. At length he relaxed his grip on the dead creature's neck. Blood squirted from the stump in a pulsing stream. He used the bird as a paint brush to make a stylized cross of blood over the desktop, adding frills here and curlicues there.

As DuBois worked Jake wondered dreamily if the red Vendetta 210 he had seen in the window of Blefescu's Imports would be waiting for him in the afternoon, but it dawned on him that he would never find out. His life as a millionaire had scarcely begun; now it was over. Voodoo Miracle, Inc. had been ill–prepared for a hostile takeover.

"Oh, Ghedé!" DuBois spat a bloody feather from his mouth and drew his face close to Jake's.

The Govi lid began to rattle.

"The loa likes you, Mr. Fiffo!"

Fifo, Jake thought wearily.

"He thinks you would make a fine Zombi!" DuBois began to draw the Govi closer to Jake, but stopped. Someone had knocked at the door. "Expecting visitors?" He wagged his finger in Jake's face. "A lady friend perhaps?"

Jake shrugged imperceptibly.

"Well, we shall send her away and get on with our business." The knocking continued as DuBois headed for the door. "Coming!"

Please be a cop, Jake thought. Be my ex–wife with a butcher knife and three attorneys. He watched the Houngan open the door and poke his head into the corridor.

"May I help you?" DuBois said.

The accented voice that responded was male. "Are you Jacob Fiffo?"

"You mean Fifo," DuBois said pleasantly. What can I—" He grunted suddenly and staggered along the wall. The door swung open and an oriental man wearing a white lab coat scurried after DuBois. The visitor's hand clutched what looked like a bouquet of anorexic flowers. The newcomer plucked a blossom from the bunch and jabbed it stem first into DuBois' neck. He snapped another from the bunch and plunged it into the houngan's crotch. Again and again his hand leapt to the bunch at his side then darted forward, as if dealing cards in a game of Crazy Eights. With each thrust the Houngan moaned.

DuBois crashed into a wall and caromed back toward the desk. His pants cuff snagged on a chair and he fell with a whimper alongside Jake.

Jake rolled his eyes down to look at him. DuBois was breathing heavily and his hands struggled feebly to pluck the scrawny flowers that sprouted from his neck, chest and abdomen. But they weren't flowers at all, Jake saw. They were the largest pins he had ever seen. Scores of them. Just as he began to count them, DuBois' assailant crouched alongside the fallen man.

"You should have left acupuncture to the legitimate practitioners, Mr. Fiffo," he said in what Jake guessed was a

Korean accent. He held in each hand a huge pin with a head like a black marble. "You are bad for business." He jammed the shafts into DuBois' eyes. The Houngan grunted one last time and fell still.

The oriental stood and brushed the wrinkles from his lab coat. He gazed silently at DuBois for a moment then looked up at Jake. "Who are you?"

Jake rolled his eyes and tried to waggle his eyebrows.

"You cannot speak?"

Jake blinked several times as quickly as he could.

"I am Hak Soo Kim, Acupuncturist. You are one of this charlatan's patients?" He pointed at DuBois.

Jake tried to nod, but his head only sagged to one side. He swung his eyes rapidly to his left, to where DuBois' business card lay on the desktop. He brought his eyes slowly back to the right then swept them again to the card. Again and again he swung his eyes until, finally, Kim's gaze shifted to the desktop.

The acupuncturist seemed puzzled at first. He turned back to Jake and stared for a moment then retrieved the card from the desk. He turned it slowly in his stubby fingers as he read. When he finished he looked down at DuBois and mumbled something unintelligible then shook his head. The card fell from his hands and he sat alongside the Houngan. He looked up at Jake and said, "*You* are Jacob Fiffo."

Fifo, Jake thought as he watched the acupuncturist settle to the floor in a relaxed heap.

HUNGER

Freedman turned off Route 219 at the sign for the Poelzl Colony. He stopped on the gravel road and considered driving his rusted Focus to the McDonald's he'd seen a few miles back. The pride he'd felt after skipping breakfast was gone: he was famished. The urge to turn around for a Big Mac was strong, but it wouldn't look good to arrive late for his appointment. He prodded his belly to quell the grumbling, then drove up the hill to the tree line and the Colony office. Maybe they'd have lunch waiting for him.

He parked in the shadow of a pine and plodded up the granite steps to the fieldstone building. He felt to make sure the knot of his tie was straight, and mopped the sweat from his face with a red handkerchief. The door swung inward just as he raised his hand to knock. An old man in a black suit stepped into view.

"Please come in, Mr. Freedman."

Freedman jammed the handkerchief into his sports coat pocket and followed the man to a spacious office. His host took a seat behind an immense desk and gestured to a chair in front. Freedman sat.

"I am Professor Spitalsfield, the Headmaster of Poelzl," the old man said in an indefinable European accent. He made no offer to shake hands. "Welcome. Did you bring the contract?"

41

"I brought it," Freedman replied, "but I haven't signed it yet."

"No?" Spitalsfield frowned. "Is there a problem?"

"Well, it's just that I know so little about this place." Freedman had already decided to sign, but he didn't want to look like an idiot who would put his name on a contract without at least asking a question or two. Yet it was true that he knew virtually nothing of the Colony.

Two months after mailing his portfolio he received a vague acceptance letter and a contract that Faust would have recognized. Sales of his paintings would subsidize his stay at Poelzl, and he would remain "until a mastery of the canvas is achieved, but for no fewer than three years." The document did not explain what would happen if he did not meet expectations.

His old rival Rudy Bowen had told him about the place. Bowen had spoken mysteriously—conspiratorially—about the Colony. He claimed Poelzl had changed his life. Apparently it had: the old Rudy Bowen was a frivolous, lazy painter, while the new Rudy was a darkly serious master. His work was the rage of the New York galleries.

"You'll learn all you need to know in due time," Spitalsfield said.

"But three years is an eternity! Maybe I'm not ready to make that kind of commitment."

A smile creased Spitalsfield's wrinkled face. His sharkish eyes twinkled. "The contract specifies a minimum of three years. Kunselman remained with us for five years. Oddly enough, he expressed doubts in the beginning, too."

"Goslin Kunselman? He studied here?"

The old man raised an eyebrow. "You thought Bowen was our only graduate? There have been a few. Several of the great painters studied here."

"But Kunselman?" Freedman could feel his eyes bulging. Bowen had said nothing about Kunselman. "He has no peer in this century."

"He was nothing before he came to us," the old man said, as if stating a mathematical certainty.

"But I thought he studied at the Sorbonne."

The professor sneered. "That place," he said at length, "teaches technique. Painting is more than technique—it is perception and wisdom. Don't you agree? It is the translation of life experience into a medium that forces change in the psyche of the audience. Painting is exposition of soul—not the feeble, callow soul of a middle class boy who hungers for greatness and wants it spoon fed to him, but the soul of a man who knows hard work, the soul of a man who has witnessed and experienced suffering. That," —he pointed a bony finger at the wall opposite the desk— "is painting. The Sorbonne can't teach that."

Freedman swiveled in his chair. The broad canvas hung in an alcove near the door. A Kunselman. The powerful surrealistic style was unmistakable. The painting depicted a sprawling wooden structure engulfed in flame. Torrents of red and orange rushed from the windows of the building. A central tower hovered in partial collapse amid the conflagration. Sheets of flame leapt skyward. Clouds of black smoke billowed from the inferno. Tiny blazing figures fled from the main entrance, while other fiery people plunged from upper story windows or wandered, dazed. In the middle ground, a blazing man clutched the blackened corpse of an infant in scorched swaddling and ran headlong as if to leap from the painting. His face was stretched taut in an accusing scream. In the periphery and foreground were the ghastly silhouettes of his tormentors, cadres of shadow men in black uniforms, the fires glinting off the sinister curves of their coal scuttle helmets and the hard edges of their automatic weapons. Several had rifle butts poised to greet the burning man.

"The Persecution of the Branch Davidians."

"Yes," Spitalsfield said. "One of his most sublime works."

Freedman grunted as he wriggled from the chair to approach the canvas. He fumbled in his pockets and produced a cigarette and a book of matches. After inspecting the Kunselman more closely he turned and expelled a funnel of smoke from his pursed lips. "It's the original, isn't it?"

"Of course."

Freedman nodded and puffed his cigarette then faced the canvas again. "If I could paint half so well."

"You can. Maybe better. Your portfolio is a bit thin, perhaps, but your abilities are manifest: you have more raw talent than the man who painted that."

"You really think so?" Freedman looked over his shoulder.

"It is my business to know these things." The old man waved impatiently toward the chair. "Sit. Please."

Freedman resumed his seat and ground out his Benson & Hedges in Spitalsfield's crystal ashtray. He slipped the contract from his coat pocket and scanned the pages, but his eyes wouldn't focus. "I just don't seem to have the drive, the energy." He bit his lower lip and frowned.

Spitalsfield proffered a black fountain pen. "Sign." He exposed a mouthful of thin, yellow teeth in a mockery of a smile. "We will be your drive. We will provide the energy."

Freedman took the pen and flipped back to the first page. It bore the heading "Poelzl Colony—Agreement" in large black letter typeface. "Three years is a damned long time."

Spitalsfield sighed. "Young man, our background check shows you to be an excellent candidate for us: you have the requisite talent and, as fate would have it, you are a loner. You have no friends or family to distract you."

"You investigated me?" A bubble of fear rose in Freedman's stomach.

"Of course," Spitalsfield answered. "That is how we knew you to be fat and weak and undisciplined. What you must know is that without our assistance your talent will be frittered away on foolishness. You will spend the rest of your days on the public dole or perhaps airbrushing T–shirts in the carnival sideshow. Here you can achieve greatness."

Freedman glanced at his abdomen and blushed. The fabric of his shirt was drawn so tight that pale flesh puckered through the slits between the buttons. His thick fingers quickly shifted his tie to cover the seam.

He wanted the greatness. He wanted to be mentioned in the same breath with Monet, Kunselman, Cezanne. His hunger for it had only increased once he'd learned of the Poelzl Colony. But three goddamned years? "The third year I get to paint what I want, right?"

"As stated in the contract, your third year and any subsequent years will be given to projects of your own selection—under guidance, of course. But you will also spend much of your time in the third year instructing new students. Remember, though, that the first two years will be a blend of training, hard work and painting. You will paint what and when you are told. You will earn your keep through the sale of your work and, as I said, the work will be hard. Sleep, meals, personal hygiene—every aspect of your life will be controlled by us." Spitalsfield cocked his head and scrutinized Freedman's slouched figure.

"You will hate us. You will beg to leave, but you will go nowhere. For at least three years you will have no contact with the outside world and if you graduate you will not divulge our method to anyone upon leaving this place." Spitalsfield looked sternly at Freedman. "If nothing else, you'll learn that much."

"Kunselman did this?"

"We gave him that greatness. We made him."

Freedman took a deep breath and brought the pen toward the paper, but the professor's hand darted out and clutched his wrist.

"Not yet." The old man pressed a button on the intercom.

"Yes, Sir?" a raspy voice crackled over the speaker.

"You're needed." Spitalsfield released Freedman's plump wrist. "Our notary will be here in a moment," he explained pleasantly. No sooner had he spoken than there was a knock at the door.

"Come."

Two men entered. Both wore navy blue jumpsuits and engineer boots. They might have been twins: six feet tall, broad shouldered, with fair skin and bristly, straw–colored hair. One took a position near the door, feet apart and hands behind his back. The second man stood next to Freedman.

45

"This young man has expressed the desire to become a painter, Herman." Spitalsfield tapped a finger on the document. "Kindly notarize his contract."

Herman pulled a chair up to the desk. "This is more a gentleman's agreement than anything," he said to Freedman. "Not one of our contracts has ever been challenged in a court of law. Isn't that right, Professor Spitalsfield?"

The old man barked out a short laugh. "Quite correct."

Herman sat and emptied the contents of a small leather case onto the desk–top: an ink pad, a rubber stamp and an embosser. "Go ahead," he said.

As Freedman signed each page of the contract, Herman stamped and dated them in turn. He signed each sheet and pressed his seal into the paper with the embosser then handed them over to Spitalsfield.

The old man shuffled the papers into a neat stack and slipped them into a manila folder. The folder went into the black filing cabinet behind him. "Thank you, Herman."

The notary rose and packed his case, then returned the chair to its original position. He moved to the door and adopted a stance similar to his twin's.

"Empty your pockets," Spitalsfield said. He placed a large envelope on the desk and produced a clipboard. "Your personal effects," he explained in response to the bewildered expression on Freedman's face. "They'll be stored, as will your automobile."

Freedman fished the wallet from his back pocket. There wasn't much else: some loose change, car keys, nail clippers, a penknife.

Spitalsfield snapped his fingers and held out his hand. "The cigarettes, too. Smoking is not allowed in the compound."

Freedman reluctantly placed the Benson & Hedges on the desk along with his book of matches.

Spitalsfield inspected each item and made a notation on the clipboard. When he came at last to the package of cigarettes, he shook one halfway out and extended it. "A last puff or two, yes?"

Freedman snatched it greedily. Spitalsfield lit it for him then put everything in the envelope and licked the flap. He smoothed the envelope's seal with his gnarled hands then filed it in the cabinet. He examined Freedman with his piercing shark eyes and nodded. "You have made a wise choice. Shall we begin?"

Freedman nodded and took one last drag on the cigarette before butting it.

Spitalsfield placed some clothing and a pair of battered work shoes on the desk. "You will need these. This, too." He put a thick book on top of the shoes, a red leather volume with a hubbed spine. "This will be your Bible."

Freedman gathered the things in his arms and stood. His lungs were already hungry for another cigarette.

"To the compound now, Louis," Spitalsfield said to Herman's companion.

Louis held the door and Herman stepped out onto the porch. Freedman followed, with Louis and the old man bringing up the rear. They marched down the steps and followed a flagstone path to the back of the building and into the woods. Shafts of late afternoon sunlight poured through the canopy of leaves overhead to produce the effect of golden pools in an otherwise dark sea of vegetation. An Indian summer breeze whispered through the trees and ground cover. Birds chirped. A woodpecker went about his business on a nearby tree, making a sound like a toy machine gun.

The trees soon thinned out into a meadow and the woodland sounds yielded to the noise of heavy machinery. An asphalt road ran along the east tree line, roughly parallel to the path they had taken. Two tractor trailers lumbered along the road, back toward Route 219. The trailers proclaimed in large black letters: "ART SALE OF THE CENTURY"—and in smaller print— "The Poelzl Colony." Freedman stopped to watch the trucks. The drivers waved just before disappearing into the woods.

"Soon your work will go out on trucks like those," Spitalsfield said. He gave Freedman's back a firm shove, and the younger man began walking again. Herman looked over his shoulder and flashed a smirk at Freedman before resuming the march.

A barrier lay across the meadow ahead. At first Freedman thought it must be chain–link fencing. He could see the figures of men moving behind it, but as they drew nearer he saw that it was barbed wire. His pace slowed to a shuffle then, and Louis nudged his back with something hard.

"Hey!" Freedman looked back at the grinning escort.

"Keep moving." Louis held a thick plastic baton. He jabbed it into the middle of his back a second time. Freedman gasped and walked faster.

The path ran by a sentry box just before it passed through a gate in the wire and into the compound beyond. The party halted as a man indistinguishable from Louis and Herman emerged from the box to open the gate. Several hundred yards beyond the fence was a cluster of long wooden buildings that looked like military barracks. A grimy brick structure rose in their midst like a nineteenth century factory. Its towering smoke stacks spewed clouds of soot into the azure sky.

Scores of men stood in the muddy field between the buildings and the barbed wire. Each man had an easel and seemed to be racing to finish the painting before him. A handful of tall, swaggering men in blue jumpsuits and engineer boots moved among the easels, as if inspecting the works in progress. The uniformed men carried batons.

The painters wore only baggy shorts and tattered work shoes. They were impossibly thin men, mere skeletons with scarcely a trace of muscle on them. The man nearest Freedman stopped his painting briefly, as if sensing the newcomer's gaze, and turned toward the gate. His features were more skull than living face: eyes sunken in blackened sockets, gristly depressions where cheeks should have been. The man shook his head slowly then daubed his brush on his palette and continued working.

"My God, what's wrong with them?" Freedman's voice was thick with alarm and pity as he faced Spitalsfield. "Are those men sick? They look as though they're starving."

The old man exposed his yellow teeth in a tiny smile. "Of course they're starving. Hunger produces greatness." He nodded at Louis, who immediately rammed his baton into Freedman's massive belly.

The artist snorted in pain and shambled backward. "Make him stop that!"

Spitalsfield smiled. The guard jabbed him again.

Freedman wheeled about and hurried toward the open gate.

"'Hunger was then my faithful bodyguard,'" the old man called after him. "'He never left me for a moment and partook of all I had . . . my life was a continual struggle with this pitiless friend.' It's in your book!"

Freedman scarcely heard a word. He looked up as he approached the gate and read with horrified fascination the motto emblazoned on the arch above him.

WORK MAKES YOU FREE

His trembling legs stiffened as he came to a halt below the arch. He began to shake his head, slightly at first, then with the sweep and rhythm of a metronome's pendulum. "No," he said in a soft voice, his head wagging back and forth. "No." He dropped his bundle and turned, intent on walking back up the path and away from this hellish place, but Louis and Herman barred his way.

"Pick those things up!" Spitalsfield's voice was cold steel.

Tears welled in Freedman's eyes and coursed down his blanched, fat cheeks. "No," he said, still shaking his head in disbelief. "I'm leav—"

The pain was like nothing he had ever experienced—an explosion of white light and flame that tore from the back of his legs where the sentry hit him, to the base of his skull. He fell to the ground with a girlish shriek, then Louis and Herman joined in with their batons. He writhed and squirmed beneath the rain of blows, the three guards beating his fat thighs, flanks and arms, a barrage of bone–jarring, stinging impacts that didn't stop until he had scurried to the things he had dropped.

Mewling like a whipped dog, he gathered the clothes and work shoes to his chest with shaking arms. Lastly he picked up the book. As he lifted the volume from the hard–packed dirt of the path, he saw the title: *Mein Kampf.*

And then the beating resumed.

CONTROLLER

Chessman returned to his room after another double shift at the recycling works, prepared his supper of drab vegetables from the mason jars in his pantry, and poured a cup of solar tea. He sat stiffly on his grimy plastic couch and ate, gazing at the black HD screen that covered one wall of his room.

Once the room had been cozy, back when HD was new and magical, but through the years the charm of HD waned, the couch lost its shine, and Chessman found it an increasingly tiresome place to remain. They no longer showed the films he had loved as a child and the sportscasts were gone, replaced with political lectures and Gaian documentaries.

Chessman was always too tired to read (he didn't read well anyway) and he couldn't take evening walks, not with the curfew. He might have slept but the HD wouldn't let him until the scheduled hour. The damned thing would just come on intermittently. No longer would his controller turn it off, nor could it lower the volume, and while the HD blared he couldn't sleep. There was nothing to do anymore but stare at the black screen and wait.

An hour or so after supper the HD flashed into white fuzz that quickly resolved to the smiling face of Big Jim Morphy, host of *Execution*.

"Good evening, citizens," Morphy said cheerfully. "Praise Gaia, but we've got plenty to keep us busy tonight!"

Chessman's stomach tightened as Morphy prattled. A balloon of anxiety formed in his gut and rose to his throat. Years—maybe decades—earlier Chessman had been a fan of Morphy, back when Execution seemed right and just. Then there had been plenty of evil people the community was better off without, and Chessman turned his controller dial with civic pride. Rapists, murderers, gun traffickers, and pederasts all fell at the hands of citizens.

True criminals were mostly gone now; Chessman couldn't remember the last murderer to meet his end on Morphy's show. Lately the charges were trivialities: malingering, failure to meet quota, wetland defilement, or any of various crimes against Gaia. Chessman no longer helped with executions. It was about the only thing he was allowed to decide anymore.

"Get ready to turn those dials, citizens!" Morphy exhorted.

A video window filled one corner of the screen. In it was an old man strapped to a chair, wires sprouting from the metal cap on his skull. "This human, the former citizen Remo Radon of Batavia, destroyed one of Gaia's precious coyotes as it fed. He claims to have done so in defense of his grandchild." Morphy sneered. "Coyotes are not so easily replaced as humans, citizens. Execute him!"

A vertical white bar appeared at Morphy's right side. It began to turn red from the bottom up, like a tube filling with blood.

Morphy glanced at the rising column of red and smiled. "Yes!"

I would have done just what Radon had done, Chessman thought.

It didn't occur to Chessman to hunt for his controller. He'd listened to Morphy before and helped kill people guilty of trivial crimes. But he hadn't done that in a long time, and never would again.

Radon began to writhe as electricity coursed into him. Chessman knew it wasn't enough to kill the man—if the tiny charges contributed by everyone watching *Execution* were permitted to go directly to the chair, he would die too quickly to entertain anybody. Chessman guessed the condemned was administered only an uncomfortable current while the fatal charge pooled in a reservoir somewhere. The white bar must represent that reservoir, and the red column the accumulating contributions of the citizens and their infernal dials. When the white bar was completely red the contents of the reservoir would discharge to the chair.

"Remember," Morphy said, "it's your duty." He frowned. "Turn those dials! It's the law."

The column of red rose faster. When the vertical bar was completely red Radon became as rigid as a log. Suddenly lightning shot from his eyes and ears and he disappeared in a cloud of roiling blue smoke. The cloud soon thinned, revealing a charred corpse.

Chessman stared, fascinated.

"Praise Gaia," Morphy said. "But some of you didn't help, some neglected their civic duty. You!" Morphy seemed to point straight at Chessman. "Get your controller."

Chessman jerked backward on the couch and swallowed hard.

"Our next criminal, the former citizen Boyd Springer of Albany, has repeatedly failed to employ his controller during executions … "

53

VIRULENCE

The fire against the blackness of night reminded Katerina Voss of the burning villages along the banks of the Ebola. She gazed at the television and stroked her cat's shiny black coat. "Like the Bumba Zone, Punti," she whispered in his ear. The big cat purred in response and kneaded her terry cloth robe.

The live newscast showed a roiling storm of orange flame towering over Attica's massive stone walls. October clouds reflected the prison fires in a spectrum running from yellow to purple.

"They're burning more than mattresses in there, kitty."

Punti blinked lazily and closed his jade eyes.

Katerina sipped her wine and nestled deeper into the couch. Her thumb toggled the volume switch on the television remote as the news camera drew back and focused on a network reporter. She listened as the man summarized. State corrections officials had acknowledged that a disturbance was underway among the population of the maximum security prison. They expected to have the situation under control soon. The town of Attica had been cordoned off, and a partial evacuation of residents had been effected. Beyond that, no one was saying anything.

Katerina's concentration lapsed as she watched the flames. She heard only an occasional phrase from the newsman's commentary. "Second Attica Uprising," and "societal failure," she thought he said—and something about unbridled street crime in America. Finally, she was certain she heard, "What you see is a consequence of the dehumanizing effects of chronic prison overcrowding."

Katerina's lips tightened slightly. It was the closest thing to a smile she had managed since the trial.

Attica won't be crowded much longer.

She brushed a few strands of hair from her face and lit a cigarette. The half smile broadened as she finished the glass of liebfraumilch and scratched Punti's ears.

Goodbye, Raca.

Somewhere behind those prison walls, Raca would die in a grotesque fashion. Perhaps he was already dead. Katerina glanced above the television to the spot where Danny's picture had hung. She had taken the photo down because each time she looked at it she wept. Removing it had made no difference. A familiar stab of bitter grief rose to her throat. Try as she might, she could not stop thinking about the agony and terror Danny had endured. She clenched her teeth and squinted back the tears.

Who could do such things to a child?

Through the eternity of waiting that ended with the discovery of her son's mutilated corpse, Katerina had contracted—folded in on herself like the petals of a flower closing against the night. Raca's arrest had brought no relief or respite from grief. The monster's capture only served to put a name and a face on the shapeless evil that took Danny Voss. And Danny wasn't Raca's only victim. The boy's father might just as well have been tortured and killed with his son. Katerina hadn't seen Bill Voss in months. The sight of the gentle bear of a man so much like her father, curled in a fetal ball and responsive as a lump of dough, was unbearable. She knew he would never emerge from the catatonic state into which he'd withdrawn.

Bill had identified the body.

Katerina came close to following him into the abyss. Strangely, she was saved from complete withdrawal by the man who had taken her family, for when she had finally seen the creature's mask of arrogance and malice, her hatred blossomed. Terry Raca, the sexual sadist, had unwittingly shoved Katerina Voss over the thin line that separates the savior from the destroyer.

Goodbye, you dirty bastard.

She exhaled a funnel of smoke and peered at the grainy image of the blazing prison. Katerina knew what was happening within those walls. She had seen it before. Her eyes lost focus as the old images of Ebola Yambuku's work crowded her mind.

☐

Nothing in medical school or in her field experience as a virologist had prepared her for Zaire. Nothing she had ever studied or heard or dreamed had readied her for Kinshasha and the Bumba Zone.

Before Yambuku appeared, Katerina had seen hundreds of deaths resulting from one plague or another: typhoid, Machupo, Lassa fever, Breakbone. But the brown, yellow, and black faces that paraded before her might as well have been cartoon characters for all the empathy they commanded. She lost no sleep worrying about the Thai children who fell before the scythe of dengue, nor did her appetite fail when she thought of the Indians decimated by Machupo. She never thought of these hapless, simple people as human. Her fight against the viruses was like the challenge of the logic problems and jigsaw puzzles she and her father had once joyously labored over. These people were merely colored pieces on a table, numbers in a sudoku.

Her dispassion was somehow linked to her father's death, she was sure—as if his passing had in an indefinable way killed *her*. Certainly happiness had died with him, for life seemed nearly purposeless to Katerina after he had gone. She abandoned her dream of becoming a pediatric oncologist and drifted instead into the safely emotionless field of virology. It was less painful, after all, to look into the screen of an electron microscope than into the face of a dying child. She buried her father and finished her residency, then buried herself in her research with the Tropical Medicine Institute. In order to keep her professorship she was required to work in the field. She left the laboratory reluctantly, but quickly found that she had developed an indifference toward death. She did not think of her own mortality at all, and was unaffected by the deaths she witnessed.

The Institute was one of three research facilities that traditionally responded to the World Health Organization's calls for containment teams when deadly viruses emerged in Third World countries. Katerina and her colleagues would fly to a hot zone, quell the contagion, then leave. She never really got to know the people she helped. She couldn't speak their provincial languages. They weren't her friends. She had nothing in common with them except the same biological vulnerabilities in the face of the self–replicating, molecular machines. The virus–stricken people were no more than elements in a riddle. Yambuku changed that.

It was the latest mutation of the prototype virus Ebola, that took its name from the Ebola River, the banks of which were first scourged by it in 1976. Yambuku produced the same nightmare symptoms of the earlier hemorrhagic fever but had a shorter incubation period and killed ninety–five percent of its victims. There was no cure. No antitoxin, serum or antibodies had yet been developed that would stay the course of the disease once its symptoms appeared. Worse still, it was an airborne contagion: when Yambuku's victims coughed, they expelled clouds of aerosolized droplets of mucous and saliva that carried the virus to the next host.

An innocent cough may have infected Sofia Galiardi in the '93 outbreak. The pert epidemiologist had been Katerina's assistant since her training in Belgium, and had accompanied the virologist on every containment mission. Katerina respected and needed Galiardi for her technical and linguistic abilities, but more importantly, she could not do without the epidemiologist's humanity. Galiardi felt for the black and brown and yellow people what Katerina Voss did not. She saw them for what they were: people. People in a different world, to be sure, but people just the same, with loves, fears, and expectations not fundamentally different from those of the Western scientists. Katerina knew these things, but did not *feel* them. Kind as a saint, but unyielding as a sergeant of marines when necessary, her American friend served as interpreter and emissary to the world Katerina was too busy saving to understand.

☐

They met the U. S. and British teams in Kinshasha's shanty town district where square miles of rickety shacks of scrap wood and corrugated iron had erupted with Yambuku. The virus had come to the capitol from the devastated Bumba Zone, the region along the Ebola River where jungle yielded to savanna. Those fleeing the rural areas had brought the plague into the impoverished city and it spread like a brushfire. The airport was closed and the city was cordoned off by government troops to prevent the infected from traveling. The streets ran with blood and fear, from the virus and the violence it spawned. There was no shortage of fire and looting. The dead and dying lay everywhere, while those seized by terror or the psychosis caused by Yambuku struggled to flee or hide. The containment teams constituting the World Health Organization's relief mission quickly recognized that they had been sent on a fool's errand.

The Westerners withdrew from the city and made their encampment on a grassy, sun—bleached knoll in the Bumba Zone. It was here in the field hospital that they treated refugees from the hundreds of villages that had been burned to stay the course of the plague. Much of their energy was spent on grave digging.

The horizon blazed at night with the flames of newly torched agricultural settlements. When a villager became infected, his family and neighbors isolated him in a hut, passing food and water in through an opening cut in a wall. If after two weeks the victim did not emerge, the villagers burned the hut. The Bakongo people had for generations used this simple yet effective technique in the fight against smallpox, but it had done little to slow the spread of Yambuku. The daytime sky was gray with smoke and there was always fire at night.

The scientists worked to gather blood and tissue specimens from survivors to isolate antibodies and synthesize a serum to inoculate those not yet infected. They hoped to increase the survival rate to fifty percent. But after two weeks on the Ebola River, their labors far from complete, the Westerners themselves began to die. Despite their Tyvek suits, respirators, and gloves, as if disdainful of their sterile technique, disinfectants, and paranoiac's caution, Ebola Yambuku came for them.

Sofia Galiardi died a month after the Belgian team's arrival from Antwerp. Four days of wracking headaches and diarrhea accompanied the persistent cough and fever that signaled her doom. She knew, of course, what to expect, having seen thousands of victims, yet she did not weep or complain. She lay down on her cot in the stupefying equatorial heat and waited.

On the fifth day blood clots formed throughout her body and she suffered a series of paralyzing strokes. The parietal and occipital lobes of her brain were damaged, leaving her blind and demented. She forgot who and where she was. Her utterances were reduced to recitations of the catechism she had learned as a girl in the Buffalo Diocese.

And she sang.

Katerina had never heard such beautiful singing. In a weak yet clearly trained soprano, Sofia Galiardi sang on her deathbed the ariettas and madrigals of her Catholic youth. She stopped speaking altogether and sang nearly continuously for two days until her voice was reduced to a grating croak as hemorrhages erupted throughout her body. Her skin flared with a coarse rash, and bruises appeared wherever she was touched by the gloved hands of the nurses and physicians. The bedding had constantly to be removed and burned as virus–laden blood gushed from her distended colon. The intravenous puncture sites made to administer plasma and antibiotics bled uncontrollably, and Galiardi's now horrid singing was choked off intermittently as she vomited black sludge.

Ave Maria was the Galiardi's final song. In the end, her voice became a feeble rattle that reminded Katerina of the warning clicks of a Geiger counter. She died of shock as her weakened veins and arteries burst. She coughed great bubbles of red saliva. Lymph thickened with broken corpuscles leaked from her eyelids, nose and ears. The mosquito netting was damp with blood from the rupturing of tiny vessels at the surface of her skin. The sheets were red. The cotton ticking of her mattress was red. Her face was red.

Katerina Voss supervised Galiardi's autopsy and saw to it that the liver sections and blood samples were properly taken and packaged for shipment to the biocontainment laboratories in America and Europe. Afterward she wrapped Galiardi in sheets soaked with sodium hypochlorite and placed her inside two zippered mortuary bags. She buried her friend just outside the WHO encampment.

Just as her father's death had killed some vital element of Katerina's personality, Galiardi's tortured passing resurrected it. For years she had plodded along a desensitized path that left her unmoved by the deaths of scores of strangers. It was as though she had been an observer of life rather than a participant. When Galiardi died the sense and urgency of being alive flooded back upon her. She saw clearly what she had been blinded to before, that she was human like all the rest: helpless in the face of dengue, Machupo, Yambuku. Helpless before Death. Katerina understood as she wept over the grave of her friend that the anguish and grief she felt was exactly what had been felt by the thousands of Bakongos they had tried to help. She shared much with them now, especially the overwhelming drive to forestall death. For the first time she was afraid for her own life.

Fear mushroomed to panic as the virus spread quickly through the ranks of the containment team. Katerina packed her few belongings, and loaded one of the team's Land Rovers with enough water purification tablets and food for a month–long stay in the bush. She took Sofia Galiardi's tissue samples, carefully packing the screw–top containers in double bags doused with disinfectant. She fled the encampment at night with the blazing horizon at her back as she drove from the plague. Katerina spent three guilt–ridden weeks on the savanna waiting for her own symptoms to appear. When nothing happened, she made her way to Kananga Airport and returned to Belgium.

She resigned her position with the Institute and moved to the United States to accept a position as chief medical officer at Syntox Labs in Rochester, not far from Galiardi's childhood home. She would supervise the production of serums and vaccines. The job paid well and carried none of the risks she had been exposed to in the past. Despite her professional caution, she kept Galiardi's tissues.

Yambuku lay dormant in the basement freezer of her suburban home, securely locked in vacuum bottles. Imprisoning the virus might be as close as she could ever expect to come to defeating it, but she planned someday to thrust the beast under an electron microscope and study it. Someday, when the horrible memories had dimmed, she would try to find a way to neutralize it.

Someday never came. Katerina married and had a child. For six years she was happy, more content than she would ever have imagined possible. More alive than she had ever felt. Then Terry Raca found her. Just as Death had found her father, just as Yambuku had found Sofia Galiardi.

Like some inexorable natural phenomenon, Raca emerged from the shadows and destroyed all that was precious to her. Like a tornado out of a blue sky, like a virus out of the pristine rain forest. A virus.

Raca killed Danny Voss and destroyed his father, and a putty–brained judge sentenced him to only six years. If it had been a life sentence, or if the creature had not so obviously enjoyed having his exploits recounted at the trial, Katerina might have returned to the kind of living death she endured after her father had died. But only six years? A mere six years, after what he had done? Back out into the world after only six years to torture and kill some other family? No. Raca had butchered an innocent child and broken a fine man. Nothing was left to Katerina Voss, nothing but a virulent hate.

With six years to plan, she took only a day. She thought of Yambuku and wondered if it could be used against this new virus, this Raca. "The enemy of my enemy," she remembered her Alsatian grandmother was fond of saying, "is my friend."

Terry Raca, meet Mr. Ebola Yambuku, late of Zaire.

It was simple enough to introduce her two enemies. Her plan entailed some risk, though she wasn't afraid for herself. Her only concern was that Raca be destroyed. What happened to her or anyone else as a consequence mattered not at all.

She had saved enough money to buy the discreet services of a helicopter pilot, a taciturn Gulf War veteran she had found on the Internet. They flew in an unmarked chopper from a private field in Monroe County to Attica, and hovered over the prison's four exercise yards in turn while Katerina pitched out cases of cigarettes. As expected, droves of inmates converged on the bounty. They made a second pass and dropped cases of liquor. Salted in with real whiskey bottles were some Katerina had filled with the Yambuku serum cultured in her makeshift basement lab. The bottles were packaged in such a way that they burst like shaped charges on impact with the ground, sending billions of aerosolized droplets into the air.

It was easy. Predictable. The prisoners rushed to their doom like starved pigs to a trough. Like a virus to its host. And what were these felons but a plague to be stayed in its course? Katerina did not care that four or five thousand prisoners would die—they were all Racas. Let Yambuku visit them, embrace them, improve them. She was unmoved by the certainty that Yambuku would find the prison guards and their families, and the people of the town of Attica. Their despair, when compared to that of the multitude of past and future victims of the contagion held within the prison walls, did not dissuade her. It was unfortunate, but a greater good justified their sacrifice.

The virologist wasn't greatly concerned that Yambuku would extend its bloody reach beyond the town of Attica. Even the second rate medical people at the prison had sense enough to begin a quarantine once the first severe symptoms became widespread in the inmate population. And if it <u>did</u> somehow

63

make it to Buffalo or Syracuse or Rochester? What of it? So long as Raca died, nothing else mattered. And Raca would almost certainly die—either by the disease itself or from the terror–fueled violence behind the prison walls. She remembered Kinshasha .

Goodbye, Terry Raca.

□

She glanced once more from the television to where her son's portrait had been. The tears came again as she tried to picture Danny's smile, but all that entered her mind were his terrified screams. Then she thought of Raca's face—the dark, lifeless eyes, the perpetual smirk and the sallow complexion, his flesh like that of some creature evolved in darkness. She tried to imagine that face in the agonals of Yambuku. A bloody face. The Masque of the Red Death. Only Poe had prophesied the Ebola strains, and in his grim laudanum visions penned the warning that came to mind whenever Katerina remembered Zaire:

"Blood was its Avatar and its seal—the redness and horror of blood."

The drone of the reporter ended and the scene shifted to the stairs outside a New York City courthouse where another journalist began his story. Katerina poured a fourth glass of lukewarm wine and lit another cigarette. This was her second day camped out in front of the television. She was waiting for something, but what? She wasn't sure how she'd know that Raca was dead, yet she watched.

"What was that, Punti?" Something the newsman said caught her attention. He had called somebody lucky.

"They are being housed temporarily at Ryker's Island until the rioting at Attica is suppressed. Most of these convicts were brought to New York just days ago to give testimony in pending criminal prosecutions or to be retried on appeal."

The camera zoomed in to the courthouse door as a troop of manacled prisoners in orange jumpsuits filed out. Katerina's stomach knotted and a chill rippled up her spine as she glimpsed the face of the third man to shuffle down the courthouse steps. There was no mistaking those dead eyes. Terry Raca directed his arrogant grin at the camera, ready as ever to caper for an audience, but he frowned suddenly and rubbed his forehead. His normally pallid cheeks were flushed.

He coughed.

What will New York be like a month from now?

Katerina shrugged and leaned back in the couch. She exhaled a cloud of blue smoke and butted her cigarette. She turned down the television volume and watched as the image of the burning prison returned to the screen.

"And Darkness and Decay, and the Red Death," she said to Punti, scratching the black cat's chin, "held illimitable dominion over all."

Punti purred.

CAN MAN

Santiago saw the Big Bag Lady die. He'd needed to stretch his legs, to get away from the heap of claim folders on his desk, and found himself standing at the window, gazing down six floors to Main Street. Can Man was there: a lanky brown man in a soiled Bills jacket and longshoreman's cap, propelling his battered grocery cart through the driving rain. Santiago had seen him close up many times and guessed him to be at least sixty years old, yet Can Man moved with the energy and purpose of a young wolf.

Can Man differed from the other street people. He wasn't a wandering cigarette–and–change scrounge like the plainly schizophrenic old woman with indecipherable hieroglyphs shaved in her fuzzy scalp. He never sat listlessly like the one–legged man in the wheelchair, waving a paper cup at passersby, mumbling curses at those who offered no alms. Can Man had a schedule. Can Man worked for his food.

The white collar crowd that lunched on the hotdogs and soft drinks sold by the sidewalk vendors usually thinned out after one o'clock. That's when Can Man would appear, ranging from the Metro engine shops near the foot of Main to the black hole seven blocks north where the rails dropped steeply into the subway. He would work up one side of the street and down the other,

67

bolting from one trash receptacle to the next, snatching discarded cans and bottles from them with his spindly arms.

Usually his cart was filled with five–cent cans when he came back down the street, but bad weather sometimes kept the office workers indoors and then his haul would be poor. Once during a February storm, while waiting for a train beneath the shelter at the last street–level platform, Santiago saw Can Man pushing his cart up out of the subway like some mutant groundhog on a shadow hunt. The steel basket held a meager gathering of cans, but there were several parcels—three or four odd–shaped items wrapped in black plastic trash bags and tied neatly with twine. It was a bad day for cans, but the scavenger had been able to find something of value anyway, though what was in the bags Santiago couldn't imagine. They weren't the right shape for cans. They looked heavy.

"Hey, Can Man!" He was curious and called out impulsively. "Find something good?"

The scavenger ignored him; his face was an expressionless mask and his eyes didn't so much as twitch toward Santiago. But that was typical Can Man. He spoke to no one and ignored every pedestrian he encountered. Everyone—the shoppers, the merchants, the errand boys—ignored him, as well. Everyone, that is, except the other street people. They shunned him. If he approached on one side of the street, they would cross quickly to the other. They would take refuge in the foyer of the nearest building when their paths crossed, as if afraid that Can Man's enterprising labor might be contagious. The accordion players, the preachers, the psychos—the homeless dregs of the city—all kept clear of him.

Can Man was not one of them.

☐

"You'll go hungry tonight, Can Man," Santiago whispered sadly at the emaciated figure as it neared the garbage can opposite the Church Street Metro platform. There weren't even enough cans in the guy's cart to finance a cheeseburger, and there were only a few steps left on his route.

The Big Bag Lady stood a few feet from the garbage can, unprotected in the wind–tossed rain, staring up at the blackened sky. Many times Santiago had seen her standing like this, oblivious to the weather, clutching a huge, lumpy purse to her breast, gazing skyward.

She looked down as Can Man approached at his usual brisk pace. The wind blew her hair out behind her like so many gray rat tails as she faced the scavenger. She dropped the purse then, and her arms came up as if to fend off a blow. She shouted something, but Santiago couldn't make it out over the loud clanging of the bell on the electric train just then rolling down the tracks.

Can Man began to accelerate as if racing the Metro, and the woman backed hurriedly from the trash can toward the platform across the street. To Santiago it appeared that the scavenger turned and stared at the woman, but it was difficult to be certain from where he stood. She pivoted suddenly from her backward shuffle and broke into a run—just turned and ran like a spooked rabbit. But the train was already between her and the platform, and though she immediately threw her arms back and tried to plant her feet, it was no use. Her sneakers failed to grip the rain–slick asphalt and she slipped feet–first under the wheels.

The train screeched to a halt and the Big Bag Lady slumped against its rear truck like a sack of rubbish. She may have screamed when her legs were sheared off, but Santiago didn't notice. The beating of his heart was like a drum in his ears and the stale office air rushed into his lungs with the sound of ripping paper.

Santiago watched as Can Man abandoned the grocery cart and sprang toward the Big Bag Lady. Halfway across the street he reached up under the back of his Bills jacket and yanked out something long and black.

"Go, Can Man!" Santiago shouted, thinking the scavenger had tugged off his belt to use as a tourniquet. "You can . . .

The cheer of encouragement died on his lips as the black object unfurled in the wind.

It was a plastic trash bag.

MR. CALDER'S THUMBS

On the way back to Sunday school with Miss Perez's books, Betty and Isbel took a short cut that brought them to the front lawn of the courthouse. They lay down on the freshly cut grass with their heads beneath the hedge bordering the sidewalk, and gazed across Ossining Street to the village square, to the box that held Mr. Calder.

The pair of benches that usually occupied the center of the tiny park had been removed, and in their place was a wooden box about the size of the church organ. Mr. Calder's head and hands protruded from holes in one end of the box. A foot or so in front of him was the stone pedestal of a bird bath, the marble basin of which had been replaced with a large glass jar. His head was immobilized in a leather collar similar to the yokes worn by the draft animals that worked the fields outside the mine belt. The restraint kept him from turning away from the jar.

"All right, we've seen him," Isbel said. "Can we go now?"

"Shhhh! Somebody's coming." Betty pointed furiously in the direction of the storefronts lining Main Street.

A big, dark–haired man in a narrow–shouldered blazer with overlong sleeves was walking toward the church on the far side of the square. His left hand gripped the sling of the automatic rifle hanging from his shoulder, and his right arm swung briskly at his side. He came to a halt just short of the church steps and turned to face Mr. Calder.

"It's Mr. Corcoran," Isbel whispered. "He'll see us. Let's go!"

Children were not permitted near the square during punishment. Ordinarily, Isbel would not have dreamed of breaking the rule, but Betty had insisted on coming here—that's why she had volunteered them to fetch the new prayer books Miss Perez had forgotten to bring from home. It seemed safe enough; on a Sunday morning all of the grown–ups except the sentinels on the village perimeter would be in church. But here was Johnny Corcoran's father. Isbel was afraid.

"He's not looking at us," Betty said.

Mr. Corcoran walked to the square and stood about ten feet from the box. He looked at Mr. Calder for a moment, then raised his head as if to gauge the weather. His jaw began moving—he seemed to be talking to the white clouds that rolled slowly above the budding maples lining the square.

"What's he doing here?" Betty frowned as she stared through the opening between the gnarled hedge trunks. "He's late for the service."

"He's praying, I think," Isbel said, calmer now that she knew they hadn't been seen. As if to confirm her guess, Mr. Corcoran crossed himself. The air throbbed suddenly with the bass tones of the church organ, and Isbel recognized the chords of "Rise Up, O Men of God."

Mr. Corcoran looked at his wristwatch, then pivoted and hurried across Main to the church. He paused on the steps and scanned up and down the street, and across the square. The girls ducked instinctively as his glance swept along the courthouse hedge. When they looked up again, he was gone.

Betty turned to Isbel and twisted her face into a disbelieving sneer. "You don't suppose he was praying for that bastard—"

"Betty!" Isbel looked quickly about to make sure no one else had heard. Ten year old girls were not supposed to talk like that.

"Why would he pray for that bastard?" Betty smiled defiantly.

"He crossed himself." Isbel could feel her face burn, though from embarrassment or anger she wasn't sure. Betty was always trying to shock her, and usually succeeded. "He was praying—you saw. Maybe for Mr. Calder. I don't know."

Betty rolled her eyes and snorted. "Why would anyone pray for him? He stole something from Johnny, and now he's being punished. I just wish I knew what he took."

"Me, too, but nobody knows—nobody but the grown-ups."

"Savannah Livingston almost found out," Betty said. "She told me her parents talked about it the night everybody heard the screams in the ice house. She didn't get much of what they said—just that Johnny was missing and that Mr. Corcoran found him in Mr. Calder's curing shed. Later that night she saw the constables drag Mr. Calder to the blacksmith's shop. Saw that with her own eyes. She knew they'd caught another thief 'cause Mr. Corcoran followed the constables with a branding iron."

"But that was months ago." Isbel's brow crinkled and she cocked her head. "When they cut off a thief's thumbs they set up the box the next day—punishment always starts the next day. Why did they wait until yesterday to put him in the box?"

"Well," Betty said, "maybe they messed up when they cut his thumbs off, or maybe Mr. Corcoran burned him too much when he stopped the bleeding. Yeah—I'll bet they froze the thumbs and waited for him to heal before they punished him proper."

"Maybe. But Mr. Calder was never punished before that I know of. They only cut things off thieves who don't stop after the whippings. He was never whipped."

The girls exchanged puzzled looks.

"Maybe he did something worse than stealing," Betty suggested after a moment. "But if it was something really terrible they'd have hung him, wouldn't they?"

"*Hanged*, stupid." Isbel rolled her eyes. "I don't know."

"Maybe it was a kidnapping!"

"I don't think so. I think they'd just kill anybody who did that."

They looked toward the square again.

Isbel wondered what it would be like to be a convicted thief, to be imprisoned in the box with nothing to look at but the jar that held her thumbs. Of course, she wouldn't want to look at her own severed thumbs withering in the sun and would close her eyes, but she didn't think anyone could keep her eyes closed forever, and the way the jar was positioned it would be difficult not to look at them. Perhaps she could roll her eyes away from the jar, but eyeballs tire quickly with such work and eventually point straight ahead. She shuddered. Poor Mr. Calder.

"Miss Perez will wonder why we're taking so long. She'll kill us if she finds out we came here. Let's go." Isbel stood and brushed the grass clippings from the front of her dress. She picked up her carton of books.

"Scaredy cat," Betty said. "We have lots of time. Let's go look at the thumbs. Then we'll bring the books back—she'll never know."

"What?" Isbel could scarcely believe what she'd just heard. "You said we'd look at Mr. Calder. You didn't say anything about thumbs."

"What can you see from here? A box with a head sticking out of it. I want to see the thumbs, don't you?"

"No." All Isbel wanted to do just then was go back to Miss Perez's classroom. She wanted to see the new prayer books that had been brought back to the village from the latest raid on the City. The books were almost certainly pre–Crash, and she loved everything that had been made before civilization fell. The last thing she wanted to do was go to the square. She shook her head. "No. You're the one who wants to see the thumbs—you go. I'm going back to Sunday school."

"Chicken."

"Maybe. But I don't see you going anywhere." It was true. Betty still lay propped on her elbows beneath the hedge.

"I'm going!"

"Then go." Strangely, Isbel was no longer concerned about Miss Perez or the books or Sunday School. She was too fascinated by the change in her friend—all of the toughness and brass seemed to have vanished from her. Betty was always daring people to do things, always leading other kids into trouble, always getting punished. But never alone, Isbel knew. Betty never did anything alone. She suddenly realized that Betty was afraid. Afraid to go to the square by herself, afraid to risk anything alone.

Isbel knew then that she was free of her friend's taunts, that she could lead rather than follow. She immediately tested her new role by saying what she had heard so often herself: "Scaredy cat."

Betty's face reddened and her lip trembled, but she did not move. She just stared into the dirt beneath the hedge. "Am not," she said in a small voice.

"I'll go look, then." Isbel placed her carton of books on top of Betty's. "You coming?"

Betty slowly shook her head. Now that her fear had blossomed, it seemed, she was rooted to the earth.

Isbel could scarcely believe she was going, let alone going by herself. But she'd said it, and now she must do it. Things had changed between her and Betty. To back out now, without seeing the thumbs, would cancel that change.

She worked her way along the hedge until she came to the gap where the courthouse drive met the sidewalk. She stuck her head out around the corner of the hedge and looked up and down Ossining Street. No sentinels were about; there was no movement along the storefronts on Main Street, nor at the church across the square. The only sounds were the rustle of leaves in the wind, and the muted voice of Reverend MacLane delivering his sermon.

She took a deep breath and ran across the street to the square. When she reached the side of the box, she was gasping for air and her heart was pounding.

Mr. Calder must have heard her, because he groaned then. She backed away from the box and hunched down, shuffling to her right until she could see his head and hands. His short gray hair was ruffled, like he had just crawled from bed, and his unshaved face was pale. He was staring at the jar.

Suddenly his eyes shifted toward her, and a burning tickle rose from her stomach to her throat. In that instant she realized that he could tell others she'd been here. Why hadn't she stayed out of sight? She could have seen the thumbs from the side of the box and Mr. Calder would not have seen her. Now she was trapped by this old man's wild–eyed stare.

"Sin no more," Mr. Calder croaked.

"Huh?" Isbel didn't understand at first. Then she remembered the admonition given to those who were punished. She swallowed, and it felt like she'd eaten dust. She licked her lips and said, "Yes, Mr. Calder. 'Go and sin no more.' They'll let you out of there soon." She smiled, but she felt sick.

The man tried to nod, but the leather collar held his head firmly. He looked back at the jar and groaned again—a nasally sound that reminded Isbel of a veal calf.

"They'll let you out of there soon," she repeated. Then she looked at the jar, too. For a full minute she gazed at the open glass container, and the swarm of flies that buzzed around it. Finally, she turned and examined Mr. Calder's hands.

"No more," he said, this time without looking away from the thing before him.

The church organ hooted out the strains of "I love Thy Kingdom, Lord," and Isbel's stomach began to heave. She held her breath and stopped her throat so she wouldn't vomit. Slowly at first, then faster and faster, she backed away from the jar. After only a few yards she whirled about and ran back to the courthouse.

Betty was waiting for her behind the hedge, with the boxes of prayer books at her feet. "Did you see his thumbs?" she asked.

Isbel reared her head back and tried to slow her breathing.
"Well?"

Isbel gulped and nodded. "Yes," she said. She picked up her box and walked quickly toward the rear of the courthouse.

76

It would take a while to circle back to the classroom behind the church, and Miss Perez was waiting.

Betty lifted the other box and hurried after her. "Were they crawling with maggots? Were they bloody and disgusting?"

"No." Isbel kept walking. Already her breathing was returning to normal; already the horror of Mr. Calder's punishment was fading. And Betty was following.

"Well, what did they look like? Were they frozen?" Betty sounded disappointed.

"They looked like thumbs, scaredy cat," Isbel said with a mischievous grin. "His thumbs looked perfectly normal."

Betty ran ahead and walked backward in front of Isbel. "How can somebody's thumbs get chopped off and still look normal?"

Isbel laughed and veered around Betty. She quickened her pace and called back over her shoulder, "They didn't cut off his thumbs!"

SPEED

The day after losing his second Boston Marathon to Reignbos, Marasigan visited Robin Goodfellow, manager of Gehenna Bioengineering. Goodfellow reached over an onyx desktop to shake hands. "How can we help you, Mr. Marasigan?"

Marasigan sat down and blurted, "I want my face redesigned."

"You're already handsome."

Marasigan blushed. "With this flat mug and these ears sticking out like sails? Come on—you've seen prettier chimps. But who cares about looks? I want speed."

"Speed?"

"I'm a top marathon runner, but I don't have the body to win big races. I train maniacally, but it doesn't make up for my short stride. I can run all day, but not fast enough to beat Reignbos."

"Rainbows?"

"Jason Reignbos. He beat me in college then bumped me off the Olympic squad. Two years now he's won at Boston. I'd do anything to beat him."

Goodfellow smiled. "I understand."

"I need a design I can take to a plastic surgeon. Maybe pin back these ears somehow, chisel the bones and push everything forward—a hatchet face to lessen wind resistance. Anything to cut my time."

"Winning means that much?"

"No. Beating Reignbos does."

Goodfellow tapped his computer keyboard. A printer at his elbow spat out several sheets of paper. "Would you like to beat Reignbos' best time to date on any course?"

Marasigan's jaw dropped. "With a facelift?"

"No." Goodfellow laughed. "More than that. You'll have your hatchet face and longer legs. Maybe a little something to increase efficiency. Old Harry downstairs has eons of experience; he'll redesign you. Our contract surgeons and therapists will see that the operations and recuperation go smoothly. Our attorneys will make certain no modification violates race rules. The organizers will seek injunctions to prevent you from racing, naturally, but the attorneys will—"

"Excuse me," Marasigan interrupted, "but Michael Jackson couldn't afford this. I've got only ninety grand."

"We don't want money."

"What then?"

Goodfellow fished the papers from the printer and handed them to Marasigan.

Marasigan read them quickly and grinned. "You're kidding, right? My soul?"

"Think about it, Mr. Marasigan," Goodfellow said pleasantly. "The contract describes the procedures in exacting detail, from bone splicing to relocation of musculature. Who else could have anticipated your needs and prepared a contract so speedily?"

Marasigan re–read the contract. "I beat Reignbos. You get my soul. No cash?" He chuckled. "Gimme a pen."

Goodfellow obliged him. "We guarantee you'll beat Reignbos' best time to date."

"Where I come from, that spells 'victory.'" Marasigan scribbled his name. Then a puzzled look crossed his face. "What's this about wings on the last page?"

"They'll reduce drag and dissipate heat."

"I'll look like a hood ornament!"

"You'll be efficient, fast, and devilishly handsome."

□

Marasigan had an arrowhead profile and flat, pointed ears. The transplantation of four–inch sections of his humeri to his femurs made him look like a thalidomide nightmare. Fused thoracic vertebrae canted his torso in mantis fashion, but assured the optimum angle of attack into resisting air. The wings had been seeded with Marasigan's own tissue at a Massachusetts lab, then grown over polymer scaffoldings mounted on an immunosuppressed pig. Red surgical scars webbed his body.

He looked like a bat out of Hell.

Marathon officials lost the court battle, as Goodfellow promised, but the judge directed that he start dead last in the pack—despite his second–place finish the previous year.

On race day they made him await the starting gun in a tent. When the race began, an official lifted the canvas flap. Marasigan emerged. Spectators shrieked as he flexed his wings and began to run.

The pack fell before him like rioters before rubber bullets. Runners looking over their shoulders gaped in horror and bolted from his path. Panicked men and women ran in all directions, screaming and stumbling.

An hour after he cleared the pack Marasigan began to pass strong runners. Some gave him bewildered, startled looks. Others seemed blasé. All tried to keep pace with him, to no avail. An hour later he passed a cluster of world–class competitors. Ahead of them was a solitary runner.

Reignbos.

Marasigan closed quickly, at a pace well ahead of Reignbos' best time ever. As he pulled within several strides of him Marasigan bellowed, "Reignbos!"

Reignbos looked back. His face contorted into an expression of abject terror. Instantly he turned and sped toward the finish line faster than Marasigan or anyone else had ever seen him run—as though the Devil himself were chasing him.

NIMBY ONE

When the main door of Mount Weather's ground control station opened, Harding turned from his monitor to watch the President enter. Harding stood and stuffed an unlit cigar into his mouth then smoothed the wisps of gray hair on either side of his otherwise bald head. He nudged the chief flight engineer with his elbow. "Show time, Pizetzner."

Pizetzner swiveled toward the door. "Sir," he said after a moment. "She struts like MacArthur promenading across the deck of the Missouri on VJ Day."

Harding smiled. "Only she doesn't smoke a corncob pipe."

"True," Pizetzner said. "And MacArthur didn't wear skirts." He turned back to his display. "—so far as anyone knows."

Like MacArthur, President Willa Newcomb usually traveled with an entourage of toadies, but today she was accompanied only by two Secret Service turret heads and her Press Secretary, Ms. Mann. A C–Span commentator, makeup girl, and camera man followed close behind.

The President stopped abruptly before the central bank of monitors and switchboards that dominated the room. The turret heads halted on either side of her and stood poised to deal with any threat that might present itself. They scrutinized the dozen or so flight engineers and technicians seated at their stations along the walls, and glared finally at Harding.

Harding extended a meaty hand to President Newcomb. "Dick Harding, Ma'am," he said gruffly, "Mission Manager. Welcome to Nimby Control."

The President accepted the proffered hand and squeezed it firmly, if briefly. "Thank you, Mr. Harder—"

"Harding."

"Harding, then."

"We have just enough time for the whirlwind tour, Ma'am," Harding said. "If you'll just—"

"That won't be necessary, Mr. Harding. Would you excuse me for just a moment?" The President waggled her fingers at her Press Secretary. "Anita. The speech."

Mann rooted around in her bag and handed over several sheets of paper.

"All right, then," the President said as she scanned the text. "Two minutes before *Nimby One* leaves orbit, the camera rolls. I announce that a solution to the nuclear waste problem has been found, and that my administration is proud to have played a significant role, and so on, et cetera. On cue I press the button that starts the spacecraft's engine. *Nimby One* leaves orbit and heads for the sun with its cargo of radioactive trash. I pause for a moment of silence then remark on the pleasant irony of a President pressing a button for a peaceful application of nuclear power. Lastly, a two sentence wrap up: thank you and good night, my fellow Americans, and so on, et cetera." She looked up at Mann. "Then what?"

Mann yanked an iPad from her bag and tapped the screen several times. "Philadelphia. Tomorrow, 9 A.M. Ladies' Garment Workers convention. The Glass Ceiling speech."

"I hope you've freshened that one up a bit."

"It's a brand–new piece, Ma'am."

The President nodded. "Let's get this over with. Mr. Harding?"

"Step this way, Ma'am." Harding took the President by the arm and escorted her toward the podium. As they passed the central console the senior OMS programmer swiveled in his seat. "Better hurry, Madam President," he said in a quavering voice. "*Nimby One* will break out of orbit in five minutes."

Harding slowed to glare at the man.

The wiry programmer pursed his lips and blinked slowly through his thick–lensed spectacles.

"No, Mr. Greene," Harding said. "Fifteen minutes."

"Five, sir."

"Fifteen."

Greene's spectacles made his eyes appear the size of half dollars. "Four minutes, thirty–eight seconds," he stammered, and offered a gap–toothed grin.

"This is not the time for jokes, mister," Harding growled. "Mind the telemetry."

Greene, still grinning, turned back to his control panel.

Harding led the President to the Podium. "When I give the signal, press this," he said, indicating a red button mounted on the upper surface of the podium.

"What's my cue?"

Harding snapped his right fist forward and flipped his thumb up.

"What if I botch the timing?" The President licked her lips.

"Timing's not much of an issue, Ma'am." Harding shifted the cigar from one corner of his mouth to the other. "The button merely authorizes the onboard computer to fire the main engine. You'll press it at least a few seconds before the programmed firing can occur. There'll be a small delay, but it will appear that you've actually fired it."

"Isn't that cheating?"

"No, Ma'am. If you don't press the button, the engine won't fire—it can't fire. You will be authorizing it." Harding checked his wrist watch and glanced at the countdown chronometer on the wall. "We've now got thirteen minutes before the OMS re–orients the spacecraft."

"Two minutes, sir," Greene called out.

Harding yanked the cigar from his mouth and shook his head.

85

The President frowned. "Who is that annoying man?"

"Greene is our token annoying little man, Ma'am," Harding answered. "Class clown. Practical joker. But the best damned OMS programmer in the country."

"OMS?"

"Orbital Maneuvering System—a series of low–thrust rocket motors that will get *Nimby* pointed in the right direction for her breakout."

"One minute, thirty seconds," Greene said.

Harding ignored him. "You'll be able to see it on the shuttle camera monitor." He pointed toward the panoramic video display on the wall to the right of the podium. "*Excelsior*'s crew unloaded the contents of the last Emergency Re–entry Module several hours ago. They'll record the breakout before returning to Edwards Air Force Base."

The President tried to look at the display, but the C–Span makeup girl had begun to dust the shine from her face. After a moment of ducking and craning, she shooed the girl away.

Harding stuffed the soggy stump of his cigar back into his mouth and gazed at the display.

Nothing was happening. The gleaming white structure of *Nimby One* just hung in the blackness of space. It reminded him of a milk bottle rack connected to a pepper mill. Instead of milk bottles, however, the ungainly spacecraft carried hundreds of cylinders packed with radioactive waste: spent fuel pellets, low–grade plutonium, medical garbage. Fifteen thousand tons of hot trash that nobody wanted in their back yard.

Suddenly the control room filled with the pulsing honk of an alarm horn. Yellow lights began to blink on the telemetry station panels and the room pulsed red with flashes from gumball machine fixtures on the ceiling.

Harding rushed to his station and flopped into the seat. He turned to Pizetzner. "Report."

Pizetzner yanked the communication headset from his ears and faced Harding. "We have a problem, sir."

"Tell me something I don't know, Pizetzner."

The chief flight engineer flipped a switch on the panel before him. The image transmitted by *Excelsior*'s camera appeared on a console monitor. "Look."

Nimby One slowly rotated. Tiny spouts of white vapor shot from the sides of the pepper mill; the spacecraft's low–thrust attitude motors were firing. Suddenly the larger orbital adjustment thrusters flanking the main engine nozzle flared bright delta vee burns. *Nimby One* moved off–screen.

"Shit," Harding said to no one in particular as the shuttle camera panned to track the ship. The thrusters had stopped firing, either by design or lack of fuel. "Look at that. The main engine nozzle is pointed outward. If that thing fires she'll come home like a goddamned buzz bomb!"

"It won't fire unless the President's authorization button is pushed," Pizetzner said. "If we had enough time, *Excelsior*'s crew could manually turn her around and reset the onboard computer for an unprogrammed firing. If we had time."

Harding drew eyeball–to–eyeball with the chief flight engineer. "What do you mean, if we had time?"

Pizetzner wrinkled his nose and leaned back in his chair. "Well sir, we no longer have complete telemetry, but it seems the thrusters have changed the spacecraft's course and dropped her into a rapidly decaying orbit." His eyes darted to a nearby terminal display of ground station tracking data. "We've got maybe three hours before she hits the atmosphere. And—"

"And?"

"And the main engine is losing fuel."

A crowd of flight engineers and technicians had gathered behind the two men. Everyone's eyes turned to the image of *Nimby One*. A plume of pale fog had sprouted from the spacecraft's fuel container petcock. The plume fed a rapidly growing cloud.

"Jesus Christ." Harding spat out his cigar and began to rub his temples furiously. "Somebody kill that goddamned alarm!"

Almost instantly, the horn fell silent and the red warning lights stopped flashing.

The President, ashen–faced, suddenly appeared at Harding's side with Mann at her elbow. "What is it, Mr. Harding?"

Harding lowered his hands and whipped up a lopsided smile. "A minor malfunction, Ma'am. Would you excuse me for just a moment?" He turned and searched the surface of the nearest control panel until he found the sodden remnant of his cigar. He crammed the thing into the corner of his mouth and shouted out of the opposite corner. "Hollis!"

A chunky woman in a white lab coat just a shade whiter than her round face squeezed between Harding and the President. "Sir?"

"Get *Excelsior* on the horn. Tell Captain Kildenny to close on *Nimby*. They'll have to suit up for an emergency EVA. Pizetzner will give you the proper vector. Move!"

Hollis elbowed her way back through the crowd.

"Mr. Harding!" President Newcomb's look of sick fear had vanished. She wore a *don't you dare ignore the Commander in Chief* expression. "This is clearly more serious than a minor malfunction."

"Look, lady," Harding snapped, his face twisting into a malevolent scowl, "if I stop to chit–chat with you now, our minor malfunction will become a major league clusterfuck."

The President's eyes widened and her lower lip twitched.

Harding's expression softened. He took a deep breath and exhaled slowly. "I'm sorry, Ma'am. Just let me get a handle on the situation, okay?"

President Newcomb nodded almost imperceptibly.

"Thank you." Harding quickly scanned the control room. No one but Pizetzner, Greene, and Hollis were at their stations. The rest of the control room crew were gawking at the shuttle monitor. "People. Back to work."

The technicians and flight engineers stumbled over one another in their haste to return to their consoles. Harding turned back to Pizetzner. "Whose station controls the propellant latch valves and petcocks?"

"Greene has the fuel transfers on this mission, sir. He covers OMS and the main engine fuel and oxidizer supplies."

Harding gnawed his cigar. "Greene! What in Hell is going on with the goddamned fuel supply?"

Greene stood and said, "It's jettisoning, sir."

"Why is it jettisoning, Greene?"

"Because I programmed the onboard computer to do just that, sir." Greene smiled affably. "We are now minus one minute, forty–three seconds to terminal orbit injection."

Pizetzner moaned and buried his face in his hands.

Harding's mouth worked silently. His cigar dangled from his lip for an instant, then dropped to the floor. At length he took a deep breath. "Have you lost your mind, Greene?"

"No, sir." Greene climbed up on his chair and stood precariously. He tugged a wad of paper from his pants pocket and, squinting, began to unfold the rumpled sheets several inches in front of his thick spectacles.

Pizetzner looked up. "Oh, Christ, sir, he's going to make a speech."

Greene began to read in a loud, cracking voice. "On behalf of the Stewards of Gaia, I hereby declare this mission a crime and insult to the Earth Mother, a testimony to man's inherent evil—"

"Somebody, please remove this crazy son of a bitch," Harding said. "Before I kill him. Get a security team in here!"

Two technicians seized Greene by the arms and hauled him from the chair. His feet hit the floor with a thud, but he clutched his speech close to his face and kept reading, even as they dragged him toward the door.

"—and malignant disposition. Better that man's folly end here and now with the death of several millions—"

Pizetzner picked up a red phone and punched a code into the handset.

Just then Greene tittered loudly, "Gaia will heal in time, and man will learn the lessons of his folly—"

Suddenly the room was flooded with brilliant white light.

Harding shielded his eyes. "What the—"

Pizetzner cupped his hand over the phone. "The C–Span crew, sir."

Harding scooped his cigar off the floor and flicked a speck of dirt from the business end with his index finger. He scowled and strode toward the door. The C–Span commentator had already positioned himself between the camera and Greene, but before he could raise his microphone to his mouth, Harding knocked the video unit from the cameraman's shoulder. He stomped it with both heels until its flood light went out, then he ripped the microphone from the commentator's fist. "Sorry, folks," he said, smiling around his cigar. "No interviews today."

The commentator stood and sidled over to the cameraman. The makeup girl joined them just as the steel door of the control room hissed open. Four wary MPs with M18s drawn darted into the room.

Harding pointed at Greene. "Gentlemen, that man is a saboteur. Kindly lock him up."

One of the MPs holstered his pistol and grabbed Greene's speech.

"You cannot stop it!" Greene shouted. "The Stewards of Gai—"

The MP silenced Greene with a choke hold.

Harding spat a chunk of tobacco at the feet of the C–Span crew. "And get these chuckle–headed bastards out of my sight. Oath 'em: They are to forget everything they may have witnessed here today." He jammed his finger into the commentator's chest and followed up with a few savage pokes. "You and your crew are about to swear an oath of secrecy. Failure to do so will result in a long stay in the Hot House."

The newsman cringed under the assault of Harding's finger. He crept backward, a look of shocked bewilderment on his face. "Hot house?"

"Leavenworth," Pizetzner called over his shoulder.

Harding jerked his head toward the door.

The security team hustled Greene and the C–Span crew out of the room. The steel door closed with a phlegmatic sigh.

"Mr. Harding," Pizetzner said. "*Excelsior* is in position."

"Hollis! Talk to me!"

"*Excelsior* is standing off *Nimby*, and awaiting instructions, sir!"

Harding gave her a thumbs–up. "Pizetzner, where are we at with this decaying orbit?"

"The OMS and main engine transponders are kaput, but we've got the redundant position telemetry back on line. It's consistent with our ground tracking station data. *Nimby* has an orbital inclination of 31 degrees; she should start to break up in the atmosphere about two hours from now."

"Where's she coming in?"

"Tough to say exactly."

"Say inexactly."

"She'll start to burn somewhere southwest of Galveston and, depending on how much skipping she does in the thicker air, may not impact until she reaches London."

"London?"

"Great Britain, sir."

"Jesus Christ! Patch me in to Glynnis." Harding marched back to his seat. He settled in his chair and donned the communications headset. Glynnis Kildenny's voice crackled into his ears.

"What's the score, Chief?" Kildenny was all business—a Navy fighter jockette with three kills over the Med.

"*Nimby* is going to crash and burn on the heads of a lot of civilians. We need you to disable her thrusters, manually turn her around, and fire the main engine." Harding slurped his cigar. "Can you do it for us, Captain?"

"Virgillio and Sambasa have been suited up and waiting in the cargo bay for five minutes."

"Get 'em going."

There was a pause on *Excelsior*'s end.

"Glynnis?"

"Where do you want us to point her, Chief?"

"Out."

"Out?"

"Away from the planet at the most advantageous vector, Captain." Harding spoke in a strong, measured voice. "If you can get *Nimby* pointed in the right direction, and if there's enough fuel left to get her up to escape velocity, she ain't coming back."

"We're on it, Chief. Out."

Harding removed his head set and switched off. "Pizetzner, what's the fuel situation?"

"Greene's program shut down the transponders so we're getting no data on that yet. I'm uploading code from the original program to fix that."

"Estimate."

"Well, sir," Pizetzner said, "the petcock is a passive system—without an external pump the fuel is just boiling out of the container through a fairly small opening." He paused to fiddle with his slide rule. After a moment he shrugged. "We may have enough fuel left to get her on a one way trip out."

Harding gazed at the shuttle monitor. The bulky white figures of Virgillio and Sambasa where already clambering over the structure of *Nimby One*. "The EVA team should take no more than twenty–five minutes to turn her around. Assume thirty minutes from now. What will that leave us with?"

Pizetzner deftly thumbed his slide rule and scribbled on a note pad. "The probable minimum rate of boil–off would leave enough fuel for a seven minute delta vee burn. The worst–case boil–off rate would leave maybe a two and a half minute burn. I'd guess somewhere toward the higher end of that range."

"What do we need to send her out?"

"Six minutes, sir."

Harding and Pizetzner exchanged poker faces.

"I feel lucky today," Harding said. "I think we'll have at least six minutes. Keep working on the program code—if nothing else, it'll give you something to do while we wait." He folded his arms and slurped his cigar, then directed his attention to the shuttle monitor.

"Mr. Harding." President Newcomb approached the Mission Manager. Mann, as always, remained in stationary orbit about her.

"Yes, Ma'am?" He met her questioning gaze and smiled around his cigar.

"Is everything now under control?"

"We'll know as soon as *Excelsior*'s crew finishes turning the spacecraft around."

"What will happen if *Nimby* One crashes?"

Harding snorted and slipped the cigar from his mouth. "Why, fifteen thousand tons of radioactive waste will land on someone's head, Ma'am. Not to mention what's left of *Nimby* herself."

"Surely that would be no more disastrous than an airliner crash. I mean, aren't the Emergency Re–entry Modules designed to withstand atmosphere friction and high–velocity impacts?"

"Yes, Ma'am, they are. The ERMOs were designed to do just that. No question—their titanium–and–composite heat shields can withstand even a small nuclear explosion." Harding raised his hands in a half–shrug. "But they won't do us any good."

"Why not?"

"Because they're in a warehouse at Cape Canaveral."

"What?"

"The ERMOs are used only to transfer radioactive materials to high parking orbits. The few we have were used and re–used dozens of times on Falcon flights to fill *Nimby*'s waste cylinders. They were intended to contain the payloads in the event of launch explosion or mid–flight abort, not to burn up in the sun. Cost–effective, Ma'am, and safe. No one anticipated sabotage."

The President gasped and slumped into a vacant chair.

Harding looked distastefully at the slimy black lump that had been his cigar, but tucked it back into the corner of his mouth. He watched the shuttle monitor as Virgillio—or was it Sambasa?—clamped the last of six Emergency Thruster Units on *Nimby One*'s superstructure. When the astronaut gave a thumbs–up, Harding couldn't tell if it was meant for him or Kildenny.

The astronaut's backpack propulsion unit flared a luminescent orange and the puffy white figure floated off–screen. A moment later a second astronaut whisked by.

"Any luck with the engine reprogramming?" Harding cast an anxious look at his chief flight engineer.

Pizetzner shook his head. "Too many lines of code, sir. It's up to the EVA team."

"Leave off with it, then, Pizetzner. It looks like they've finished now anyway." Harding checked his watch. "Twenty–seven minutes. We may just make it."

"Mr. Harding!" Hollis's voice was excited but controlled. "Captain Kildenny is on the line."

"Put her on conference."

Kildenny's voice came through clearly on the public address system. "Chief, the ETUs are reorienting the bird now."

The monitor brightened as puffs of vapor shot from *Nimby* One's milk rack. The spacecraft began to rotate against the pitch black background.

"We took advantage of *Nimby*'s momentum, Chief. This baby's going out." The speakers crackled. "Main engine firing in one minute, forty–three seconds." There was a screeched hiss as Kildenny switched off, then back on. "Virgillio and Sambasa are in the cargo bay. We're outta here, Chief."

Nimby One moved quickly off screen as *Excelsior* thrusted to a safe distance. It took less than a minute for the shuttle camera to adjust to its new position, then *Nimby One* reappeared on the monitor.

"Thirty seconds," Kildenny said.

The President touched Harding's elbow.

"Cross your fingers, Ma'am." Harding gave her shoulder a reassuring pat. "Pizetzner, you did remember to bypass the President's authorization circuit, didn't you?"

"Did it when I wiped Greene's program, sir." The chief flight engineer flipped a switch and the countdown chronometer

94

appeared superimposed in the corner of the shuttle monitor. "Ten seconds, sir. Eight."

Suddenly the exhaust nozzle of *Nimby One*'s main engine flashed blue like a propane torch and the spacecraft receded into the distance. Flight engineers, technicians, even Mann and the Secret Service turret heads broke into unrestrained applause and cheering.

Harding, President Newcomb, and Pizetzner looked on in silence.

"That's a delta vee burn," the chief flight engineer said after a moment. "One minute, twenty seconds, and counting, sir. Go, baby, go."

A handful of technicians copied Pizetzner's farewell. "Go, baby, go."

By the time *Nimby One* shrank to a tiny white dot on the black field of the monitor, the entire room had taken up the chant. "Go, baby go!"

When the burn reached four minutes, Harding himself silently mouthed, Go, Baby, go.

"Four minutes, twenty–seven seconds, and counting!" Pizetzner shouted over the collective voice of the control room crew.

"Go, baby, go! Go, baby, go!"

At five minutes, thirteen seconds, the countdown chronometer stopped ticking off elapsed time. The room fell silent.

"Flame out!" Kildenny's voice barked over the public address system. "At five ten post–delta vee." There was a pause. "Did we make it, Chief?"

Harding slipped the pulpy slug of tobacco from between his lips and pitched it at the monitor. It stuck there like a snail.

"Chief?"

"Close," Harding said. "Close." He reached inside his blazer pocket and extracted a fresh Corona. He peeled away the cellophane wrapper and shoved the new cigar into one corner of his mouth. From the other side he said, "Have Edwards bring you home, Glynnis. Thanks. Good job. Out."

"Out, Chief." The public address system crackled and went dead.

Mann broke the silence in the room. "I have a good feeling about this," she said.

The President shot her an incredulous look.

"Your administration saves the planet from a disaster laid for you by your predecessor. This'll make great copy. Here's how we'll spin it: a press release—"

The President silenced her with sneer, then faced Harding. "It *is* going out, isn't it?"

"In a manner of speaking, Ma'am."

"Mr. Harding, please don't bullshit me." The President's voice once again sounded like a President's voice.

Harding turned to his chief flight engineer and raised an eyebrow.

"What goes up, Ma'am," Pizetzner said, "must come down."

"Meaning?"

Pizetzner hung his head and stared at the console before him. "*Nimby* has broken out of a terminal orbit and adopted a ballistic trajectory."

The President shifted her gaze back to Harding. "You said *Nimby One* was going out. Out to where?"

"Well, Ma'am," Harding said between puffs on his unlit cigar, "she's going out, but then she's coming right back here."

"Here? Mount Weather?"

"Maybe, Ma'am. Earth, anyway."

Mann whined softly.

Harding and the President both scowled at her. She fell silent.

"How much time do we have, Mr. Harding?"

"Hopefully enough time for you to authorize emergency funding for an intercept mission to send her to the sun where she belongs."

"How long do we have?"

"Hard to say exactly, Ma'am," Pizetzner said.

"Inexactly, then."

The chief flight engineer quickly consulted a telemetry display and whipped out his slide rule. He grabbed a pencil and scribbled on his pad then returned to the slide rule. Finally, he stuck the pencil on his ear. "Seven weeks."

The President turned to Harding. "And if we can't intercept it—can't send it to the sun?"

Harding slipped the cigar from his mouth and licked the business end. He grimaced, spat a tidbit of tobacco on the floor, and cleared his throat. "Well, Ma'am," he said, "then I hope to Christ it doesn't land in my back yard."

THE CHARGES AGAINST HIM

In the time it took George Mason to drag himself from his cell to Tesla Room No. 23, his morning despair dissipated. It was replaced with a calculating hate and renewed determination to crank out his sentence ahead of schedule. *Two thousand eight hundred kilowatt hours to go*, he thought. *Fifteen months. Maybe less if I work harder.*

He rang for admission then sat on the floor and stretched his legs. A moment later a section guard appeared at the window of the security booth. He looked sleepy and irritated, but buzzed the steel door open. Mason hopped to his feet and entered the room. As he headed for his Tesla generator in the front row he saw that the Four Horsemen were already there, pedaling at their usual brisk pace. Grim, uncommunicative men, they were there every morning when Mason arrived, taking up half the last row of generators. They pedaled as a team, sometimes encouraging one another in soft voices scarcely audible above the growling whine of the machinery. When he had first seen them nearly twelve months earlier, Mason had immediately thought of the apocalyptic riders of the Book of Revelation, and had nicknamed them accordingly.

Mason hung his towel over the crossbar of his Tesla and watched the Horsemen for a moment. They returned his gaze without expression. One of the four, a wiry, brown–skinned man in the far corner of the room nodded. Mason still thought of him as Strife even though he had long ago overheard one of the others call him Washington. He seemed to be the leader of the group. Strife's gesture was the closest thing to a greeting Mason had ever gotten from any of them.

Mason returned the nod and mounted the Tesla. He shoved his feet into the stirrups and flipped the power switch between the handle bars. The black display of the controller flickered luminescent green. A glance assured him that the selector knob was turned to *Sentence* and not *Lottery*. One morning following a Lottery, he had wasted an hour pedaling with the knob in the wrong position. Now he always checked before starting.

When he slipped his thumbs into the print identification sockets and gripped the handlebars, his name and the kilowatt hours remaining on his sentence appeared in bright green characters in the middle of the display. A small box in the upper right indicated energy output in watts. Another box in the upper left recorded pedaling time. His legs began to move, and the wattmeter rose quickly from zero to one hundred. As his muscles adjusted to the strain, he increased the speed until the display held steady at two hundred fifty watts.

Mason began pedaling at 5:35 A.M. He would stop for breakfast at seven, then return at 7:30 when the less–motivated prisoners trickled in to work at their kilos. Then he would increase his output to three hundred fifty watts until breaking for supper, after which he would work on the Tesla until he was exhausted, finally dragging himself back to his cell to rest up for the next day.

And the next.

On the pretext of stretching his legs, he sometimes dismounted and strolled around the grid of forty–eight Teslas, sneaking glances at displays. His wattage was consistently twice that of most prisoners, but then not many men in his section seemed overly concerned with leaving Monroe soon. Nearly all of them showed tremendous enthusiasm for pedaling on execution days, however. Mason scoffed at the Natso philosophy that supposed prisoners who helped punish other offenders somehow facilitated their own rehabilitation. He and everyone else at Monroe knew that prisoners did not mount the Teslas on execution days to reform themselves—they pedaled for a chance to win the Lottery.

Mason calculated the average prisoner's output at about two kilowatt hours per day. His own sentence would have taken nearly seven years to work off at that rate, but his production was more than five kilowatt hours per day.

Only a few men worked on the Teslas every day, and only five —Mason and the Four Horsemen—routinely stayed more than eight hours. From the day the Horsemen arrived at Monroe they were the gauge by which Mason judged his own performance. Their example helped him achieve a level of physical conditioning he hadn't thought possible. Already he was outperforming two of them, though he had a long way to go to match Strife and the brawny white man he'd nicknamed *Pestilence*. They regularly pedaled at four hundred watts or more and produced about seven kilos each per day.

Mason was sore and exhausted most evenings when he dismounted his Tesla, but the Horsemen would still be pedaling. Even late in the day, Strife and Pestilence worked at a grueling pace, though the pudgy young man Mason wryly thought of as *Famine*, and *Invasion*, a weasel–faced man with pale flesh and tattooed forearms, were more often reduced to token pedaling.

He often looked back at the Horsemen as he worked, sometimes increasing his pace as if they were pursuing him; the little game helped the hours pass and made the pedaling easier. They rarely took much notice of him, but this morning was different. When he turned his head to get the pace, they were staring at him. He quickly swung back to his display and saw that he had unconsciously increased the wattage to nearly three hundred. Screw the pace, he thought, and settled back to two fifty.

He felt their eyes on his back, and wondered briefly if they had some mischief planned for him. It didn't seem likely. If they were interested in sex, well, there were weaker, easier victims. Besides, men diligently working off their sentences— "paying their debt to society"—had no time to waste on brawling.

Mason had fought only once since arriving at Monroe Federal Correctional Facility—a brief affair that ended when section guards immobilized him and his attacker with glue guns. The fast–drying plastic goop had been hell getting out of. The unlocking solvents left a painful rash that took weeks to heal.

He glanced over his shoulder again and immediately turned forward, his heart beating faster. They were still staring at him. *You won't rattle me*, he thought, and forced himself to look back once more. His gaze shifted from Strife to Pestilence and back again. *What's your game, you bastards?*

Strife looked at the floor and continued pedaling with the same powerful strokes, his legs working up and down like brown pistons.

"George Mason," Pestilence called out suddenly. "Are you going to play the Lottery tomorrow?"

Mason turned, trying not to look surprised. At length he asked, "Do I know you?"

"No," Pestilence responded. "But we know *you*."

Mason did not look away despite the cramp building in his neck. His jaw muscles tightened and his legs slowed to ease the strain. He was prepared to fight or flee, should either action prove necessary, but until then he wouldn't flinch at mere words or a stare. "And how is that, friend?"

Pestilence ignored the question; instead he turned to Famine. "Zinchenko?"

Famine—Zinchenko—aimed his round face at the ceiling and closed his eyes. "George Mason," he said in raspy, high–pitched voice. "Widower. No close friends or relatives. Trained as a bookkeeper. No employment prospects on release. Charged June '37 with three counts of criminally negligent homicide and two counts of unlawful weapons possession. March '38, acquitted of homicide. Convicted on the weapons charges. Sentenced to five thousand kilos."

"Anyone can read the Web," Mason said curtly. It was all accurate. He had returned home from work one evening to find three kickdowners raping his wife. He killed them with the AKS rifle his father had bequeathed him. The Court ruled his action justifiable homicide, but took exception to his use of a long–outlawed firearm. Marissa slashed her wrists shortly after his trial. He would never be sure if it was because of the violence she had endured, or her grief over losing him to a Federal prison. Mason *was* sure that if he had remained a free man Marissa would still be alive.

"We've watched you for many months now," Pestilence said. "Pedaling, pedaling. A man with nothing—no one— waiting on the outside wouldn't devote himself to grinding out the kilos unless there were unfinished business in the works." He bit his lower lip and nodded thoughtfully. "We figure you've got an appointment with a judge—perhaps a prosecutor—in a year or two."

Mason cast an alarmed look about the room.

"Don't worry—the place isn't wired. The guards don't give a rat's ass what goes on in here. So long as there are no incident reports to file, and we keep feeding the grid junction in Rochester, the government doesn't care what we say or think. We're in cold storage."

"I'm just getting in shape, friend," Mason said, recovering as best he could. Still, it was bluff; he felt sick that he was so transparent, and angry that these men knew what drove him.

"Of course," Famine observed, winking dramatically. His plump torso glistened with sweat and his thick legs pumped up and down. "I'm here for the exercise, too."

Strife looked up then and smiled.

"If you want something," Mason said to him as calmly as he could, "why don't you just spit it out?"

"We want you to play the Lottery."

"What do you mean?"

"The knob on your controller." Strife's voice had a puffing, rhythmic quality. "At six o'clock tomorrow morning, turn it to the right and pedal like hell until seven."

Mason frowned. "I've got a lot of kilos ahead of me as it is and I don't care to waste any on the Lottery. Besides, I can't think of a single reason why I should help the Natsos fry some poor dumb bastard." A slim chance to win a five hundred kilo sentence reduction in exchange for diverting his wattage to the Death House seemed questionable no matter how he looked at it. Pedal for an hour to kill a man whose crime was likely no more serious than a violation of the Ozone Protection Act? Pedal for an hour without having his sentence credited for the effort? No, thanks. "Why the hell would you care, anyway?"

"It's important," Zinchenko said. "Important enough that Washington is going to play, and he's got a deadline." He jerked his head toward Strife.

"What the hell are you talking about? What deadline?"

"He was convicted of firearms distribution," Invasion said.

"I thought that carried a mandatory death sentence." Mason glanced at Strife, but he seemed not to have been bothered by the remark.

"That's true in a way," Famine said. "Condemned men are put to death only if they fail to generate three thousand kilowatt hours in twelve months. The Natsos like the prisoners' fate to rest in their own hands—maybe it helps them sleep better at night. Anyone who cranks out three thousand kilos has his sentence commuted to life imprisonment."

Mason considered for a moment. "That's impossible," he said finally. "That's more than eight kilos a day. No one can do that."

"Washington has another month to go, and he's close."

"How close?"

"*Close,*" Famine said. "If he wins the Lottery he'll make the three thousand with plenty of kilos to spare."

"And if he doesn't win?"

"He'll have to pedal harder."

Mason turned away and stretched the cramps from his neck. This conversation was interesting enough that he wanted to finish it, but he didn't want to throw his spine out of alignment talking across five rows of generators. He slipped first one foot then the other out of the stirrups and brought them up to rest on the ends of the handlebars. There was no sense wasting even a fraction of a watt hour; he kept his thumbs in the identification sockets until the Tesla's flywheel lost momentum and the pedals growled to a stop, then he swung his legs to the floor and walked back to the Four Horsemen. "Who *are* you people?"

"Underground," Famine said. "Resistance. Minutemen."

"The good guys," Pestilence added with a mock bow and the tip of an imaginary hat.

It was an awkward gesture to make while pedaling a Tesla, but Mason had to admit there was a certain elegance to it. "You must not be very good," he said, "if you ended up in here."

The Horsemen laughed, even Strife.

"That was funny, Mason," Famine said after a moment. "Very clever—but wrong. Borland here," —he jerked his thumb at Pestilence— "Curtiss, and myself were each sentenced to thirty thousand kilos for sedition. We were the bit players in Washington's gun–purchase drama; a believable cast of characters was required to lend authenticity to the operation."

"I don't follow," Mason said.

"Have you heard of Thomas Monahan?" Zinchenko asked.

"Congressman Monahan? Sure, he's the one who introduced the bill to repeal the Second and Fourteenth Amendments. The Natural Socialist bastard who wrote the gun seizure laws that brought me to this charming place."

"The very same. Our aim was to repeal him—eliminate and discredit the man without creating a martyr. He was one step away from the Presidency until we intervened last year. Thanks to Monahan and his Natso cronies there is so little left of the Constitution that nothing would have prevented him declaring himself King." Famine's round face tightened in a smirk, and his eyebrows waggled. "As it turns out, he has to settle for something less than a throne."

The Horsemen chuckled.

"Washington approached the Congressman with a compelling and quite legitimate business proposition that enabled us to set him up. An anonymous tip to the Directorate of Environmental Protection, Alcohol, Tobacco, and Firearms assured us that his telephone lines were monitored. Do you know how easy it is to make innocent conversations appear damning with a little corroborating evidence? Of course, the cryptic messages we left on Monahan's answering machine helped, as did the altered documents and the bogus files planted in his office computer and cloud folders. We even bought him a warehouse full of handguns and ammunition. Another anonymous tip led EPATF agents" —Famine pronounced the acronym *epitaph*— "to our clandestine meeting at the warehouse, and voila!"

"You sacrificed yourselves to entrap one of your enemies?"

"Exactly."

Mason grinned. "I hope it was worth it."

"It was," Strife said. "With Monahan out of the way, the Natural Socialists' day of reckoning is in sight. The lives of four men are a small price to pay to bring that day nearer. Anyway, there are tens of thousands waiting to make the next sacrifice, to win the next battle—the Movement is growing stronger every day. Join us, Mason. We need people like you."

So that's your game. "What's in it for me?"

"Restoration of the Constitution—a return to the Bill of Rights, freedom from oppressive taxation and government supervision of your daily affairs." Strife spoke as if instructing a child.

"Revenge," Pestilence added. A stern look crossed his face. "You'll need a gun when you get out. We can help with that, if it's what you really want. But a better revenge would be to bring the entire system down, not just a couple of its stooges like the men who put you here, wouldn't you say?"

"I don't know," Mason said. "I'll have to think about it."

"Play the Lottery tomorrow," Strife said. "To play is to join us."

"I'll think about it." Mason returned to the front row and resumed pedaling his Tesla.

The Horsemen did not speak to Mason again, nor did he look back at them until the end of the day when he dismounted and walked to the door on legs that felt about as steady as heated plastic. He buzzed for the section guard to let him out and wearily turned to gaze at the four riders. Strife and Pestilence seemed to be pedaling at a four hundred watt pace; Famine and Invasion were hunched over their handlebars, exhausted, yet their legs kept stubbornly moving. Finally the door opened and Mason shuffled back to his cell.

He lay on his cot for a while, thinking about what Pestilence—Borland?—had said about a better revenge. It made sense, but he couldn't understand why they were so keen on his playing the Lottery. The idea of helping the Natsos kill a man did not appeal to him. The man would surely die without his help, anyway—there were more than enough prisoners who would gladly play the Lottery even if their own mothers were wired to the Teslas.

Why did they want him to play? Was it a symbol, some sort of initiation rite? It seemed the sort of thing a pack of kickdowners would require of a prospective member: *Shoot the old man on the corner and you're one of us.*

Mason quickly tired of speculating on the motives of the revolutionaries and decided to reread Ecclesiastes, hoping it would relax him, usher him into sleep. He groped in the darkness for the night light switch and retrieved the Bible from his nightstand. It was the only reading matter permitted prisoners, apart from the *Inmate Manual.*

Impulsively he opened the book, not at the Preacher, but at Revelation, and began scanning the pages for the Four Horsemen. He couldn't seem to find them, and was about to close the Bible when a passage caught his scanning eyes. He blinked several times and read aloud in a soft voice. *"And the four angels were loosed, which were prepared for an hour, and a day, and a month, and a year, for to slay the third part of men. And the number of the army of the horsemen were two hundred thousand thousand: and I heard the number of them. And thus I saw the horses in the vision, and them that sat on them . . . "*

His voice trailed off and his eyes slowly closed. He slept then, and dreamed of revolution.

☐

Mason arrived at Tesla Room No. 23 at five–thirty the next morning. Already many of the generators were occupied by prisoners waiting to play the Lottery. He elbowed his way past the men who had not yet taken their positions and stood before the Four Horsemen. They were already pedaling. "I've given your proposition some thought," he said to Strife.

"And?"

Mason took a deep breath. "I'll join you," he said in a strong, clear voice, "because I want more than personal revenge. But I won't play the Lottery—I won't help the Natsos kill anybody."

Pestilence smiled. Strife coughed and turned away. Famine began to snigger and Invasion choked off a laugh.

"Did I say something funny?" Mason's face started to burn. He directed an angry glare from one Horseman to the next. "Well?"

At length Famine caught his breath and wiped tears from his eyes. "You've got it all wrong, friend," he said. "We're not helping the Natsos kill anyone—they're helping us kill someone."

"I don't understand," Mason said. "You—" But then he *did* understand. "Congressman Monahan?" He looked at Strife and raised an eyebrow.

Strife's face split a grin and he nodded enthusiastically.

Mason began to giggle, then clapped his hands together. At length he threw back his head and laughed. He sat on the Tesla next to Invasion and laughed even as he slipped his thumbs into the sockets and wriggled his feet into the stirrups. He laughed long and hard, and the Horsemen laughed with him.

At five fifty–five he turned the selector knob to *Lottery*. He stood on the pedals and cranked out four hundred watts for an hour and fifteen minutes—just to be sure.

GLASSPIEL

Wahn's home was a relic from the French and Indian wars —a sprawling blockhouse of fieldstone surrounded by towering poplars. Fournier knocked on the front door.

The massive wooden panel creaked inward and a prodigiously old man appeared. "Yes?"

"I'm here to see Mr. Wahn about the armonica."

"I am Eric Wahn." The old man smiled, and extended a hand. "You must be the young pianist from Chicago who called about my advertisement!"

Fournier hesitantly accepted the proffered hand and gave it a brief, awkward shake. "Joseph Fournier."

Wahn's hands resembled deformed fins, the bunched fingers sweeping away from the thumbs, their articulations swollen and red. His wrists seemed frozen at odd angles. As Wahn escorted him through a long flagstone entryway, Fournier couldn't help but stare at those hands.

"Arthritis," Wahn said. "None of the therapies has worked —gold, methotrexate, hot wax. Aspirin has done more good than anything." He laughed and waggled his fins. "But precious little."

"I'm sorry."

They entered a shadowy parlor. Wahn flipped on the lights. "Don't be—it has saved me from the madness of *this*."

Before them stood a wood cabinet not unlike a Shaker desk with treadles. Atop the cabinet, two brass cradles supported a wood spindle skewering a tightly nested array of hemispherical glass bowls. The smallest was no bigger than a tumbler; the largest could have served as a tureen. Pulleys connected the spindle to the treadles.

Fournier sat on a bench before the apparatus. "It's beautiful!"

"Yes." Wahn gently brushed a fin over the bowls. "My grandfather called it his Glasspiel. He said Benjamin Franklin constructed it, but that cannot be proved, I suppose. I have no documentation." He raised an eyebrow. "Will you play?"

"Yes!"

"Ready your fingers." Wahn produced a pan of water and placed it next to Fournier. "Soak them."

Fournier slipped his hands into the pan.

"How did you become fascinated with the armonica?"

"At the conservatory I listened to your Boston Symphony performance of 1977."

"Ah! Before my arthritis."

"Even on the school's Victorola the music was…"

"Ethereal?"

"Heavenly." Fournier shifted his hands. "I can't describe it. The music produced a resonance in my body—as if I were God's tuning fork." He shrugged. "Heavenly."

"The sound of madness," Wahn said. "You do know about the madness?"

"Yes," Fournier said. "The armonica's popularity lasted only decades because everyone who played it became ill— insane. I looked it up. The players suffered nervous disorders. But by all accounts their performances were brilliant."

"True," Wahn said. "My father played this armonica, and went mad, as did his father, and his father before him. They began by interpreting the works of the great composers, then composed new melodies and orchestrations. As the madness grew, so did their musical brilliance."

"What became of them?"

"Suicide," Wahn replied. "Asylums. The usual fates of the mad." He raised a fin. "My son the physician said arthritis saved me from such an end. Do you know what causes it?"

"Arthritis?"

"The madness."

"No."

"Lead poisoning."

Fournier cocked his head and frowned.

"This armonica—all armonicas of the eighteenth century— were made with lead crystal. The players' moistened fingers absorbed the lead. Over the years it damaged their brains. Organicity, my son called it."

"God," Fournier said. "I thought it was a curse. The literature makes the instrument sound like an evil thing."

"Science teaches otherwise—so my son told me when he was a medical student." Wahn touched the bowls again. "Still, when he returned from university, he played. He said there had to be more to the brilliance than chemistry."

"Does he still play?"

"No. He killed himself." Suddenly Wahn clapped Fournier's shoulder. "Your fingers are plump enough by now!"

Fournier dried his hands on his trousers and faced the armonica. He worked the treadles with his feet. The spindle began to turn. He touched the rim of a rotating bowl. Instantly the room filled with a vibrant hum that sent shudders of delight through his body. His fingers tested each bowl in turn, quickly measuring the range of the instrument.

"Try this." Wahn placed a score on the armonica's music stand. "Tomásek's 'Fantasie'."

Clumsily at first, then with increasing authority, Fournier played. The room swelled with throbs, whines, and a chorus of mad warbles. At length he finished the piece and cast a wide–eyed gaze at Wahn.

"Well played," the old man said.

Fournier smiled broadly.

"And do you not fear the madness?"

Fournier slowly shook his head. His feet resumed their steady pumping.

His hands returned to the glass bowls.

THE SIN OF WAGES

After dinner, Delbert Panacito slumped in his brother–in–law's recliner. He gazed out the cabin window toward the trees on the far shore of Lake Soo. He watched the fat red sun and its reflection converge. The fingers of his left hand flexed repeatedly against an encircling rubber band; his right thumb rubbed a blue poker chip held against his palm. Just before sunset he fell asleep.

Delbert woke from a smothering dream in which a grand piano was slowly crushing him. He opened his eyes with a start, his heart pounding like a drum. A lump of fear had lodged in his throat, but it quickly yielded to rage.

"Get off me, goddamnit!" He pummeled his wife's massive back with vicious punches. It was like fighting a water bed. "Get off!"

Margaret Panacito lurched from her husband's lap and retreated to the couch. The couch frame creaked beneath her as she settled into the cushions. "I'm sorry, Honey."

Delbert rubbed the sleep from his eyes then massaged his legs. He slipped the rubber band around his left wrist and rooted in the crack between the cushion and the arm of the chair until he found his poker chip. At length he glared at his wife. "Don't ever sit on my lap. If you leaned back in this chair and got stuck, I'd suffocate before help came!"

"I just wanted to snuggle. You know, like we used to." Margaret attempted a smile. "I started a fire."

Delbert glanced at the fireplace then gave his wife the smirk of revulsion he reserved for offensive strangers. She might as well have been a stranger—she didn't look much like the woman he had married twenty–five years earlier.

Margaret had been beautiful then: five feet three inches tall and one hundred fifteen pounds, with an hourglass figure that turned men's heads. Her hair had been the color of a raven, and her face a mask of wholesomeness. Now her face was an expanse of cheeks and jowls plastered with makeup. She dyed her hair brown and wore tight clothing that called attention to her leviathan body.

She withered under his gaze and began to sob.

"I'm sorry, Meg," Delbert lied. He hunched forward in the chair and forced the leg rest down. "You know I still love you." He slipped his feet into a ratty pair of slippers, then stood and tightened the belt of his bathrobe. "You know I'm cranky when I wake up," he added.

Margaret sniffled. She seemed to accept the explanation.

As Delbert looked down upon her immense body he found that the smiling got easier. He had created Meg—the chronically ill, morbidly obese Meg—and very soon the insurance companies would reward him for his patience by paying off on six one hundred thousand dollar term life policies. His smile broadened as he thought of the tremendous return on such a small investment; the policies cost a total of only seven hundred dollars a year.

His thumb resumed its habit of rubbing the poker chip; it required some effort to stop playing with the damned thing and drop it into his pocket.

"You didn't eat much," Meg said. She lit a cigarette and exhaled a cloud of smoke. "You'll get sick."

"I'll wait until after the vacation to get sick."

"Are you fishing tomorrow?"

116

"Yep." Delbert sat next to his wife. "I'll take the skiff to the mainland for two or three days. You'll be okay alone here."

"I'll be fine."

Every September the Panacitos left their children with Margaret's mother and drove up to Canada from Buffalo for two weeks on Marydale Island. The cabin they stayed in belonged to Margaret's brother, Jack, an engineer who generously permitted relatives to use his island during the spring and fall.

But Jack was always butting in where he wasn't wanted, always finding jobs for Delbert, always circling want ads and leaving them conspicuously about. Delbert loved to disappoint his brother–in–law by refusing to work. He sneered at Jack's kindliness and honesty, but always took him up on the offer of a free vacation. And every year he abandoned his wife for the company of Frank Magliucci—ostensibly to fish, though he never returned with rock bass or rainbow trout. Usually he came back with a hangover.

Delbert suddenly asked, "What time is it?"

"Midnight." Margaret wore a quizzical look; Delbert could see the wall clock just as easily as she.

"That makes it the Seventeenth, doesn't it?"

"Yes, Hon, but—"

"That means it is now officially our twenty–fifth anniversary!" Delbert yanked a large cardboard carton from behind the couch. He placed it on the coffee table and draped his wiry arm over Margaret's shoulders. "Happy anniversary."

A look of astonishment briefly froze his wife's face, then she kissed his cheek and hugged him. Tears rolled down her face, streaking her make–up, pooling black smears of mascara below her eyes.

Delbert grimaced and rolled his eyes as she squeezed him violently about his middle. "All right, already." Delbert extricated himself from her embrace before she had a chance to indulge her incessant yearning to sit on his lap. "Just open it!"

"I'm so happy," Margaret blubbered. "I didn't think you'd remember. I didn't think you cared anymore." She sniffled and dragged the sleeve of her threadbare flannel housecoat across her nose. Finally, she unfolded the four cardboard flaps covering the top of the box.

"You like?"

"I love them!" She withdrew a basket of carnations decked out with baby's breath and silver bows. She placed the arrangement on the coffee table and shoved her hands back into the carton to remove two boxes wrapped in silver paper.

Delbert tossed the empty carton behind the sofa. He watched with mild amusement as she tore the wrapping from the larger package.

"Bunnies!" It was a latch hook kit—white and pink yarn rabbits on a blue yarn field. Margaret loved rabbits and latch hook—their apartment had at least three of the things on each wall. "They're beautiful!"

Delbert straight–armed his wife to prevent her giving him another hug. She left off trying after a moment and stripped the silver paper from the remaining gift. When she saw what was inside, she frowned.

"Del. Doctor Marrier wouldn't like this." She slipped the fifth of Scotch whiskey from its red box. "I'm not supposed to drink. He said that with my weight and smoking and diabetes I shouldn't drink."

Delbert knew she referred only to hard liquor—for years now he had watched her consume three cases of Genesee Cream Ale each week without a care. "Just this once won't hurt," he assured her, flipping his hand as if to dismiss Doctor Marrier as a quack. "I'll get the glasses."

He fetched two tumblers of ice from the kitchen, then sat down and opened the Scotch. After filling Margaret's glass to the brim, he poured a small amount for himself. "To us," he said, and raised his drink.

Meg sniffled and clicked her glass against his. She tossed back her Scotch in three gulps.

Delbert sipped his and gave her a refill. He added a dollop to his own tumbler with a clattering flourish. "To my great fortune," he said, scarcely restraining a laugh, "in finding such a wife as you." He barely wet his lips while Margaret drained her glass.

"There's lots more," Del observed as he poured her another. He went to the fireplace and shoved a log into the waning blaze. The fresh wood took its place among the embers with a little encouragement from the poker. Flames began to crackle as he closed the mesh. He gazed wistfully from his wife to the heavy iron tool in his hand and back again. Reluctantly he returned it to the fireside rack and placed a stack of records on the stereo turntable. A moment later Andy Williams' "Moon River" warbled from the speakers. Before Delbert went back to the couch he retrieved a tray of cookies from the kitchen.

"I love you," he whispered into his wife's ear after he had resumed his seat. The lie came readily to his lips, though the kiss that followed required a certain resolve. Holding his breath, he grabbed Margaret's jowls and planted a lingering wet kiss on her mouth.

At length she pulled away gasping for air. "Del! What's come over you?"

"I just wanted you to know how much you mean to me," he said with calculated charm. She meant more than half a million to him. "Shall we dance?"

Margaret's jaw dropped. Delbert loathed dancing—they hadn't danced since the end of the Disco craze. "Oh yes," she said dreamily.

She dragged Delbert to the middle of the room and began to promenade him across the carpet. The flapping of slippers against their naked heels kept time with the music.

Things were going according to plan. At forty–four years of age, Delbert Panacito was about to unburden himself of wife and children—to become rich.

His needs had always been few: cable television, a comfortable chair, a bed, food, the sports pages. But in the past few years his horizons had expanded. He yearned for more than the Office of Temporary and Disability Assistance would willingly provide. The insurance money would enable him to get his own cabin and live out the rest of his days on the interest.

He might even swing a new car, perhaps even his own boat. And a TV satellite dish.

Margaret's addictive personality made planning her death a cake walk; Delbert made sure that she always had plenty to eat and drink. It had taken years, but he had gotten her weight up to the point where she tottered on the brink of physical collapse. He had spent a lot of time working for the insurance money. Now he would have it.

The Andy Williams record came to an end, and they sat down. Del's hand slipped into his pocket and began to play with the poker chip. Margaret gobbled cookies, drank whiskey, and smoked with abandon, smiling and laughing more than she had in a decade.

Delbert laughed, too.

"Let's dance to this one." Another album had begun to play—the Bee Gees Saturday Night Fever soundtrack. Margaret hurriedly butted her cigarette, then rose and extended a big arm.

The sliding, pivoting moves of the Hustle came back to her as though she'd danced them just yesterday. She moved with surprising grace for a woman of three hundred fifty pounds, but Delbert capered as woodenly as ever, clumsily dodging the hip bumps she directed at him. They danced almost nonstop for thirty minutes, by which time Margaret was red–faced and breathless.

"I've got to . . . rest," she panted. She flopped on the couch and lit a cigarette, taking one deep puff before stubbing it in the ashtray. Her upper lip was damp with sweat and her eyes were glassy; a lecherous smile crossed her face. "Delbert," she said huskily, "make love to me. Now. It's been more than a year."

"Tomorrow." The thought of climbing on top of her revolted Delbert. Still, he managed a genuine smile because he knew she never mentioned sex unless she was drunk. "Come on. Let's get you in bed. To sleep."

Margaret wore a hurt look. "Tomorrow? You promise?"

Delbert nodded.

"Okay." She sucked the dregs of Scotch from her glass and stood.

"Don't forget your insulin." Delbert had anticipated this night years before and had developed the habit of "helping" her with the injections.

"Okay. Where does it go this time—rear end?"

"Yes." He went to the kitchen for Margaret's medicine bag.

When he returned she was kneeling on the couch with her robe hiked over her back, her panties pulled down across her thighs.

Delbert cringed at the spectacle of her huge, dimpled buttocks, but he sat on the coffee table and wrapped the barrels of four insulin pens together with a strip of cellophane tape. He screwed a disposable needle on to the business end of each pen and dialed them all to the maximum dosage of 50 units. He tugged the rubber band from his left wrist and fished the blue poker chip from his pocket. He deftly secured the plastic disc to the ball of his right thumb with two tight loops of the rubber band. Finally, he wiped Margaret's flesh with an alcohol sponge. "Lift your cheek," he ordered. She did so, and he pierced the taut skin with the needles, simultaneously depressing the plungers with the blue poker chip.

"Ouch!"

"All done. Now go to bed." Delbert pocketed rubber band, poker chip, and syringes, taking care not to stick himself.

Margaret pulled up her panties and brushed her housecoat back into place. She struggled to her feet then turned and kissed him on the lips. "I love you." She gave him another rough hug and staggered off to bed.

When Delbert heard the bedroom door close, he slapped his knee and danced a little jig. "Yes, yes, yes! I'm going to be rich! I'm going to be free!"

After pouring himself another drink he hustled to the recliner. He settled into the depths of the chair, forcing the back down and the leg rest up. He sipped his Scotch and grabbed the TV remote control. When the tube flashed into life he flipped through the channels until he found a hockey game.

Delbert watched with little interest; he couldn't stop thinking about the money. The little miser in the back of his mind kept counting it. When his Scotch was finished he turned off the television and closed his eyes. For the ten thousandth time he thought about Margaret's death.

It was a splendid murder. He'd read extensively on diabetes, obesity, and heart disease. He knew that with Margaret's poor health, after so much food, booze, and exertion, the overdose had a high probability of producing death from insulin shock within a few hours. Of course, it was possible that she might linger in a coma for several days before succumbing to hypotension or cardiac dysrhythmias. But that's why he had decided to kill her early in the first week of their vacation.

In the morning he would take the skiff to the mainland and visit Frank Magliucci. The syringes would find their way to the bottom of Lake Soo along the way. He would stay with his Canadian friend, drinking and fishing several days, then return to the cottage to find his wife dead. The Provincial Police would investigate and almost certainly determine the death to be of natural causes. With Margaret's medical history, who would suspect foul play? Still, there was a slim chance she would survive. If she did, well, there was always next year.

Delbert drifted into a deep, happy sleep.

He dreamed he was in an insurance office—a surreal, glamorized place peopled with busty secretaries and darting, purposeful men in blue pinstriped suits. Delbert sat comfortably in a huge leather chair, smoking a Cuban cigar. A fawning insurance agent hugging a clipboard stood before him.

"If you would be so kind, Mr. Panacito," the agent begged, "as to sign here," —he extended the clipboard and a pen, indicating a dotted line at the bottom of a claim form— "we can give you your money."

Delbert flicked a cigar ash on the red carpet and smiled at the look of dismay on the agent's face. He grabbed the pen and signed with a disdainful flourish.

"Oh, thank you," the man said with the enthusiasm of a condemned felon who has just received a stay of execution. "Thank you, thank you," he said, bowing repeatedly as he backed out of the room through a swinging door.

A moment later he returned clutching two huge sacks of money. He heaved the muslin bags onto Delbert's lap. Delbert smiled expansively and butted his cigar. He grabbed the bags, each of which was stamped with a huge "$", and stood to leave. "It's been a pleasure—"

"But sir, there's more," the insurance man cut in. "Much more."

Delbert sat down with the sacks resting on his knees. Almost immediately the door banged open and a file of security guards marched into the room, each carrying a pair of money bags. The men laid the bags on his lap until there was no more room, then piled them at his feet and around the chair. Still more men came, bearing bag upon bag. They stacked them up to Delbert's chin while empty–handed guards trooped back through the door for more.

"Stop!" Delbert gasped. "No more, please. This is enough." His arms were pinned to his sides and the weight of the bags was making it difficult to breathe. More men came and pitched bags on and around him. All the while the insurance agent smiled and held the door open. Delbert panicked, struggling futilely against the burden of money.

"Stop," he croaked, but the money continued to pile up. Finally someone threw a bag over his face and the lights went out.

Delbert woke with a start. Dazed from the Scotch and half asleep, he opened his eyes. It was dark. The dying fire cast a faint orange glow that flickered on the cabin walls and ceiling. His heart still raced from the dream panic. He gasped for air and tried to sit up, but he couldn't move. His left arm was pinned at his side, paralyzed.

Something soft and inexorably heavy held him in the depths of his recliner. A great weight lay upon his chest, compressing his lungs. His right hand fumbled over the end table until it found the TV remote control. He pressed the power button and the cold glare of the 4:00 A.M. sports report illuminated the room. Delbert's eyes bulged in horror.

Margaret's impossibly heavy head rested on his left shoulder and her dead eyes gazed at him in adoration. She had come to sit on his lap one last time.

THE FREE AGENT

The two guards searched Murcheson as intimately as they had prior to his previous audience with Artemisa. They x–rayed his baseball and returned it to him just as Colonel Valladares, a gangly, mustachioed man wearing the standard revolutionary garb of fatigues, cap, and combat boots, arrived to escort him to the President. He frowned at the baseball in Murcheson's hand and said, "He is waiting."

Murcheson followed him up a marble staircase to Artemisa's office. Valladares opened the door and held it aside. The American stepped into the room. President Artemisa sat behind a steel desk about thirty feet away. He glanced at Valladares and nodded. The officer sighed and left.

Murcheson waited for the door to close, then rolled the baseball around in his hand, aligning the stitches with his split finger grip. He drew his left knee up to his chest and brought his throwing arm back—just as he had thousands of times on the mound in the Sky Dome. Suddenly his leg came down and his arm whipped forward. It was the same form he used to hurl one–hundred–mile–per–hour fastballs, but at the last instant his arm relaxed and the ball rolled from his fingertips in a slow pitch.

Artemisa caught the ball easily and flashed a smile.

Murcheson approached the desk. "Another gift for your collection, Mr. President," he said. "It's autographed by Luis Tiant."

Artemisa adjusted his glasses and inspected the baseball. "Thank you." He placed it in a drawer and waved his visitor to a chair before the desk. "But you have come to present your corporation's offer, have you not?"

"Yes, Mr. President." Murcheson unbuttoned his suit coat and sat. He straightened his necktie and folded his big white hands in his lap.

"Well?"

"Five hundred million dollars."

Artemisa slapped the desktop with his left hand and sprang to his feet. "It is not enough!" He snorted and pivoted to the window overlooking De Rubas Bay. "The Colombians can do much better."

Artemisa cut an imposing figure silhouetted against the blue sky. He was taller than Murcheson, and in his starched fatigues looked as vigorous as he must have been forty years earlier when he led guerrillas in the field. Murcheson liked Artemisa's brusque manner and regal bearing, and did not want to consider the alternative should they fail to strike a bargain. Artemisa had once been a pitcher, after all. One season with the Reds ten years before Murcheson was born. But Artemisa had answered the call of revolution and changed uniforms; he had forsaken baseballs for hand grenades. Now he was seventy–five years old, but he looked like he had a few good innings left in him.

"Two billion dollars," the old man said at length.

A knot formed in Murcheson's belly.

Artemisa was standing with his hands clasped behind his back, gazing out toward the Caribbean. A sea breeze fluttered his unruly beard along the shadow of his jaw. "Your corporation will pay two billion dollars and our arms negotiations with the Colombians will cease. We will 'play ball' with Nartex."

Artemisa had deferred to Murcheson's charade from their first meeting. The American was posing as a representative of the Nartex Corporation, but there was no Nartex as far as

Murcheson knew. The firm was a convenient fiction that offered both sides an avenue of plausible deniability should the deal fall through. Nick Caballo, a State Department official, had recruited him—at least Caballo *claimed* to work for the State Department. Murcheson was certain that he was really CIA, but it didn't matter. The man's sales pitch could not be refused.

The knot in Murcheson's gut blossomed into a burning tickle that rose to his throat. He didn't think Caballo would go that high. "I'll present your counter offer to my Board of Directors, Mr. President."

Murcheson wanted the deal to work; it was the path of least resistance for him. His career in the majors would continue if only he could persuade this old man to accept. His indiscretions would be forgiven and buried. No forced retirement from the game. No jail time. Artemisa would walk away with some cash for his crumbling economy, and the drug lords would have to look elsewhere for a weapons supplier. The deal had to work.

Murcheson took a deep breath. "I hope you've considered all aspects—"

"There will be no negotiation."

"But—"

"Two billion dollars," Artemisa repeated. "Convey this requirement to your . . . 'board of directors'. Return to me this afternoon at four with their response. Good morning." He maintained his pose at the window.

Murcheson stood. Colonel Valladares entered then and led him from the Presidential Palace to the limousine idling in the stupefying heat of the Plaza de la Revolucion.

☐

The government Lincoln dropped Murcheson at the Hotel Santiago. After a slow ride in a rattletrap elevator, he entered his suite and bolted the door behind him. He flopped onto the davenport that dominated the sitting room. A wobbly ceiling fan creaked overhead with each slow rotation of its blades.

On the table before him lay an oversized attaché case bearing the Nartex logo. The combination locks did not appear to have been tampered with, but he was too new at this game to be sure. His thumbs rolled the code wheels and the hasps popped open. He lifted the lid and began assembling the "ski."

The Secure Communications Environment consisted of a laptop computer equipped with a high–speed modem, a subtly modified iPod, and three pieces of dense, fibrous padding layered with metallic film. Artemisa's customs officers had looked askance at each component, especially the padding, but they had accepted Murcheson's explanation that the pieces were samples of household insulation manufactured by the Nartex Corporation. Their inspection did not reveal that one earpiece of the iPod functioned as a microphone, nor did they discover the voice encryption software on the hard drive of the laptop.

Murcheson connected the modem to the room's telephone line with a splitter and used a patch cord to link the iPod to the laptop. He booted the computer and loaded the com–munications software. Carefully aligning the Velcroed edges of the padding, he overlapped the three pieces to form a sound–deadening hood. When he had positioned the iPod headset inside the hood, he used the laptop to dial the hotel switchboard, and placed a call to a Miami exchange.

After a moment of crackling line noise, a piercing connect tone blared from the telephone receiver. He punched his access code into the laptop and pulled the hood over his head. The software began deciphering the incoming signal.

"Nartex." It was a male voice, muffled but audible.

"Pitcher," Murcheson responded. "Caballo, please." The laptop processor and hard drive were fast; the response came almost immediately.

"This is Caballo. You're skiing, I hope."

"Yes."

"Did he accept?" Caballo's voice was flat and cold.

"No. I didn't get to first base with this guy. He wants two billion."

Caballo made a noise that might have been a laugh. It sounded like a small dog's bark. "Implement Option B."

Murcheson's mouth went suddenly dry and his stomach leapt as though he had just bailed out of an airplane.

"Do you understand? *Implement Option B.*"

Murcheson took a deep breath. "There must be an alternative." He found himself wondering what kind of man was on the other end of the communications link. He had never met Caballo; their contacts had all been by cell phone calls or texts. At times he visualized the man as G. Gordon Liddy. At others, Mycroft Holmes. Today the voice fit Liddy.

"We have a deal, Murcheson. Don't bomb out on us now," Caballo said. "If this doesn't go as planned we'll hand our evidence over to the Commissioner. He'll kick you out of baseball. You'll never pitch again, unless they have a team at Leavenworth. That's where you'll end up when we've finished with you. Half a dozen Federal agencies would love to see the evidence we have against you, my friend: interstate transport of controlled substances, smuggling, conspiracy to defraud, racketeering, tax evasion, money laundering. Christ, the IRS alone will fight to get you locked in the Hot House and have the key melted. Implement Option B and you get a clean slate and the Hall of Fame."

Murcheson licked his lips and tried to blink away the stuffy darkness of the hood. What would Pete Rose or Shoeless Joe Jackson have done with this offer of redemption?

Caballo's voice softened. "What do you say?"

"You'll get me out of this when it's finished? You'll get me home?"

"That's the deal."

"Okay. Option B." Murcheson disconnected and tore the hood from his head. He quickly disassembled the SCE.

Murcheson stretched out on the davenport and closed his eyes. He'd made some stupid mistakes, and now his career—his freedom—was in the hands of a stranger. Could he trust Caballo? Probably not. A man who would stoop to blackmail would likely have no compunction about lying or betrayal. Still,

Murcheson could see no way out. Caballo had him like a fish on a hook: his fear of prison was strong, but not as strong as his fear of leaving baseball. He was a good pitcher, and had a real shot at the Hall of Fame. He would do anything to preserve it. *Anything.* He'd do as Caballo instructed and hope that he would keep his word.

Eventually Murcheson nodded off. He slept fitfully for two hours before arising to prepare for his four o'clock meeting with Artemisa. He dreamed of the Chicago Black Sox.

When he woke he felt tired and anxious, so he grabbed a stack of pillows from the bedroom and propped them against the backrest of the davenport. He selected a baseball from his flight bag and took up position near the door. After flexing and stretching his throwing arm for a moment, he began to swing it around in circles, first forward, then backward.

When Murcheson's shoulder felt loose and the arm was limber, he wound up and threw the ball. It struck the pillows with a loud *thwock.* He retrieved the ball and took five more from the bag.

Thwock.

With each throw his edginess evaporated; warming up had always calmed him down. He imagined the meter of a speed gun as he threw. It read "60 MPH" when he began.

Thwock. Thwock.

Twenty minutes later he knew his pitches exceeded ninety–five miles per hour. He was perfectly relaxed when he left the hotel.

□

Artemisa's guards frisked Murcheson and stored his personal property, then they x–rayed the baseball he had brought as a parting gift for the President. Colonel Valladares entered the security vestibule then and seized the ball from the plastic tray in which it rested. He inspected it carefully.

"Roberto Clemente." Murcheson forced a smile.

Valladares looked up and raised an eyebrow.

"It's autographed by Roberto Clemente. For President Artemisa's collection."

Valladares produced his usual frown and handed the ball to the American. "The President is waiting."

They were soon outside Artemisa's office, where the Colonel knocked on the door in his precise fashion. After a brief pause, he opened it and held it aside to let Murcheson pass. Murcheson entered the office and took up position some thirty feet in front of Artemisa's desk.

The President shuffled a pile of documents into a neat stack and set it aside. He looked up and offered a tiny smile.

When the door closed, Murcheson formed a split finger grip around the baseball. His hands came together and slowly raised the ball to his chin. He nodded then, as though acknowledging a catcher's signal, and brought his throwing arm back. His left knee rose toward the Windsor knot in his tie. It was the same form he'd used on his earlier visits to Artemisa, only this time, when the pitch came, it was a *heater*—a one hundred mile per hour fastball.

There wasn't even enough time for the old man to form a look of surprise on his bearded face. The white blur that bolted from Murcheson's hand struck him squarely between the eyes with a sound like the crack of a bat. His glasses exploded and his head snapped back, then recoiled forward, his face a mask of blood. Artemisa tottered in the leather swivel chair for an instant, then slumped onto the desk.

Murcheson stood slowly from his follow–through pose. He heard footsteps behind him, and turned to the door just as Colonel Valladares rushed toward him with a pistol in his hand. Valladares raised his arm and swung the butt of the gun down. Murcheson's head exploded with light and pain.

He fell into blackness.

☐

Murcheson's head throbbed. His eyes refused to stay focused. A narrow shaft of light poured through a barred window near the ceiling of the tiny, dank cell in which he found himself. He pushed himself to a sitting position on the stone floor and gingerly felt the side of his head. His fingers came away wet. Dried blood caked his neck and chest. The cell was cold; someone had stripped him down to his boxer shorts. He dragged himself to the patch of sunlight in search of warmth.

Scarcely had he moved when there were footsteps outside the iron door of his cell, and the sound of a key turning in the lock.

The door swung inward and the cell was flooded with light from an incandescent bulb in the corridor. He shielded his eyes with his hand.

Colonel Valladares stepped into the cell. "Get Dressed," he said, and dropped a set of fatigues and a pair of laceless boots on the floor.

Murcheson lowered his hand and looked up. "Am I going home now?"

Valladares snorted. He nudged the clothing forward with his foot. "Get dressed."

Murcheson jockeyed his arms into the sleeves of the olive drab shirt, then stood and pulled the pants up over his trembling legs. His fingers fumbled with the shirt buttons, but he managed them. Finally he settled to the floor and tugged the boots over his feet. "Is Caballo here?"

"Caballo?"

"Caballo." Murcheson grimaced—his head had found a new place to throb. His hand crept up to rub the wound. Murcheson stared at Valladares . This didn't sound right. This was not part of Option B. The Colonel striking him and imprisoning him meshed with the plan all right—for appearances' sake he supposed he had to be treated like any assassin—but they were alone now. Valladares sounded serious. More important, he *looked* serious—he didn't so much as wink. "When will Caballo come for me?"

"I do not know of anyone by that name," Valladares said.

"Come on, Colonel. This isn't funny." Murcheson's stomach rose to his chest. "You know how the plan goes, so stick to it. Don't try to scare me."

"You have much to fear." Valladares snapped his fingers and extended his arm toward the door. A guard appeared and handed him a folded newspaper. Valladares snapped it open and handed it to Murcheson.

It was *USA Today* dated the day after the final audience with Artemisa. Two headlines dominated the front page: "Artemisa Dead at 75," and "Scandal Rocks Majors." Murcheson read as quickly as his unsteady vision would allow. The former story described Artemisa's death as a result of a massive stroke; there was no mention of assassination. The latter story mentioned Murcheson's name again and again—everything Caballo had promised to suppress was right there in black and white. Murcheson's whereabouts were unknown—so the story said. He handed the paper back to Valladares . "I've been set up."

"By this . . . Caballo?" Valladares smiled thinly.

"Yes!" Murcheson's voice was shrill, pressured. "Caballo is CIA. They had all this dirt on me" —he rapped the paper with his knuckles— "they wanted me to negotiate Artemisa out of the arms deal with the Columbians. They wanted a baseball player because they knew Artemisa still loved the game and might be more receptive to negotiating with someone of similar background. And because . . . " Murcheson bobbed his open hand as if holding a baseball. "Because of the special talent involved. I was told that you and several other officers were aware of the plan and would see to my release afterward."

"Our intelligence apparatus believes you were operating alone."

"What?" Murcheson slumped to the floor. "What did you think Artemisa and I were discussing?"

"The President often met with business representatives—he took a personal interest in the day–to–day operations of government. Your visits were in connection with a public housing project. He told us nothing more than that."

"What about the arms deal with the Colombians?"

"The President said nothing of such an arrangement."

"Artemisa was about to finalize a cash deal with the drug lords. Caballo sent me to stop it." Murcheson looked up. "One way or another."

"This is so typically American." Valladares wore a look of disgust, perhaps bafflement. "You were not satisfied with the wealth generated by your baseball contracts; you wanted more, and began associating with drug dealers and gamblers. When it became clear that your illicit activities had been discovered, and that your career was at an end, you decided to Assassinate Artemisa."

"Why in Hell would I do that?"

"Notoriety. You knew you would be barred from your precious Hall of Fame. Quite likely you would spend many years in prison. What better way to ensure your place in history than by the commission of an abominable act? You've probably already signed a book contract." Valladares nodded sagely. "It is the American way. Your colossal avarice exceeds even your unquenchable thirst for fame and immortality."

"That's crazy."

"Yes, it is."

"Look," Murcheson said, "I can prove what I say." There was a note of desperation in his voice. "I came here as a sales representative for Nartex. It's a phony corporation. I made phone calls to their office. Surely you can check on that."

"We have made discreet inquiries. Nartex is an old American firm that manufactures domestic insulation materials. It is a matter of public record that you recently signed contracts with them to endorse their products."

"In my hotel room. My laptop computer has—"

"Nothing unusual," Valladares interrupted. "A spreadsheet with several files containing sales figures and product test data. Several Nartex memoranda. Commercial communications software."

"What about the voice encryption software?"

"Commercial grade."

Murcheson tilted his head back and closed his eyes. "The telephone number I called is the real Nartex number, I suppose."

"Yes. There is no evidence to support your claim. If there were, we'd have a mighty club to wield against your government." The scorn was clear in Valladares's next words. "You may have thought that you could exit in a blaze of glory by killing Mr. Artemisa, but you could not be more wrong. There will be no Hall of Fame, nor any Hall of Infamy for you. Artemisa died of a brain hemorrhage; you will never be seen or heard from again."

Murcheson was stupefied with the thought of remaining in this cell for the remainder of his life. At length he said, "When will I go to trial?"

"You have already been tried."

"Then I'm to spend the rest of my days in this cell?" Murcheson cast a bewildered gaze around the small room.

"You have already spent the rest of your life. Get up."

Murcheson stood. He had not even considered imprisonment, let alone death; the prospect seemed outlandish.

"You are to be executed," Valladares said.

"By firing squad, at dawn, I suppose."

"By necklace—now." The officer grabbed Murcheson's arm and pulled him into the corridor. "Death is waiting."

Murcheson suddenly broke free and started to run, but two guards pounced on him and wrestled him to the floor. They produced a length of rope and bound his wrists behind him, then hauled him to a standing position. Valladares walked toward the sunlight at the end of the corridor.

Murcheson was surprised at how easy it was to follow him. His legs twitched a little—just as they had before important games—but they moved, and he did not stumble. The guards gave him a nudge and fell behind him as he strode along the stone walls to a low flight of steps, then up into the tropical heat of a prison courtyard. He began looking for a gallows, but saw only a small hillock surmounted by a wooden post. The guards dragged him to it and secured his wrists to a steel eyehook embedded in the wood. They looped a second length of rope loosely around his neck and under his arms, then tied it to the post.

Colonel Valladares came to him then. At his side was a sergeant carrying a gasoline can and an automobile tire. Valladares took the tire and placed it around Murcheson's neck so that it hung from the back of his head nearly to his belly. "The necklace," he said. A thin smile curled his lips. "A little something we learned from the Haitians—a marvelous deterrent to disloyalty." The sergeant handed over the can and Valladares filled the bottom of the tire with gasoline.

Fuel splashed on Murcheson's fatigues; he felt a cold stain grow on the front of his pants and spread down his legs. He wondered if this was all part of the game, and began looking about for Caballo. But there were only Colonel Valladares and the three soldiers standing on the green grass beneath the midday sun. He was suddenly afraid and tried to dislodge the tire by tossing his head back and forth and from side to side, but the rope about his neck quickly choked him, and he gave up struggling.

"Your blaze of glory, Señor Murcheson," Valladares said. He stepped down from the hillock and nodded. The sergeant struck a match.

Murcheson's last coherent thought was that he was standing on a mound without a baseball.

THE WEIGH–IN

The afternoon of November 30th was chill and overcast—a regular nipple–stiffener. The flowers were dead and the sparse brown grass was streaked with crankcase oil. Around two o'clock, the Junkers began to gather near the office, the weathered plank–and–shingle structure between the hundred foot pyramid of hubcaps and the rusted hulk of the Caterpillar road grader. In some junk yards there were so few folks that the weigh–in took only about as long as a healthy bowel movement and didn't have to start until after four. But in this parts mecca there were more than four hundred participants, and the weigh–in seemed to take forever.

The children, more mobile than their elders, arrived first. Generations earlier they would have been sleeping or fidgeting in a classroom. Now the closest they ever got to a school was to laze around the rusted yellow carcasses of the buses their families called home. Still, they were typical kids: illiterate and somewhat less energetic than three–toed sloths. Except when it came to food. They could interpret the labels of the ancient food containers well enough, and they could run like sap for a free meal. They gathered noisily, belching and farting as they plodded lethargically along the hard–packed greasy soil in search of parking places for their massive buttocks. Their talk was of food. Always of food.

Jenny Woolsock was the first to arrive, ostentatiously displaying her father's prized barbecue fork. Other children were similarly equipped. Deke Carver, Bob Frapples and Louis DeLuise—everyone pronounced this name *DaLouie*—all prided themselves on their refined upbringing. They wielded fondue spears. The smallest children—too young to bludgeon norwoods, but sophisticated enough to gnaw bones—drooled innocently and practiced their feeding technique with plastic utensils.

The school buses bordering the debris–strewn clearing creaked ominously, their flaking yellow bodies yawing and pitching like storm–tossed ships, heralding the imminent approach of the adults. Men and women squeezed through the narrow doorways and waddled down the entrance ramps of the nearer buses, heading toward the office and the children waiting there like flightless buzzards. More grown–ups came from the hovels excavated from the junk heaps, from the furthermost reaches of the community. The men licked their lips hungrily as they surveyed their own wretched offspring and conversed absently about norwoods, trade pacts with the Grass People, and food. The women swayed humbly and gelatinously as they shuffled several paces behind their husbands, hiking their patchwork fur gowns up over their flesh aprons to avoid snagging the twisted strips of chrome body trim that sprouted from the earth like so many glittering punji stakes.

The Junkers all wore fur–strip sandals with tire tread soles. The ringing tones of briskly crossed gutting knives echoed in the clearing as the adults converged on the Scales of Plenty.

The weigh–in was conducted—as were the pelting bee, the Belchathon, and Sumo Nights—by Mr. Gordon, who had time to devote to civic activities by virtue of the fact he had inherited the bulk of the real estate leased by the Junkers. He was small as Junkmen go, weighing only three hundred eighty pounds or so. His perpetual frown and surly manner stemmed from his lifelong weight problem, it was commonly supposed, and the Junkers pitied him because he was shaped like a bowling pin.

When he arrived at the scales clad in his ceremonial norwood robe, supporting a tiny fraction of his weight with the traditional scepter (the grimy steel shaft served the three–fold function of crutch, badge of office, and roasting spit), there was a murmur of wind–breaking among the Junkers. He dismissed their protests with a wave and shouted, "Pipe down!" The constable, Mr. Wimple, followed him with the stripped chassis of a 1963 Volkswagen microbus in tow.

The assembled Junkers kept their distance, trying to elbow their way toward the rear of the crowd to avoid being selected for work, and when Mr. Wimple panted, "Some o' yous sunzabitches wanna gimme a hand wit dis buggy?" there was a general retreat until Mr. Gordon briskly cudgeled those nearest him with his scepter.

"Ow! Shit!" Mr. Holmes exclaimed, shielding his head with his massive, rubbery arms. "Okay, all right, already. Shit!" He and his rotund progeny, Mycroft, shuffled toward the constable's tow rope. They winced as they rubbed the weals on their puffy white flesh, but grabbed the rope and helped Mr. Wimple guide the weighing chariot to its resting place at one end of the Scales of Plenty. The men were red–faced and puffing when they finally kicked chocks under the wheels of the vehicle.

The original paraphernalia for the weigh–in had broken down and been traded to the Grass People long ago, and the rusted VW chassis now poised at the scales had been put into use even before Shaqueena Pickwick, the oldest woman in the junk yard, had been expelled from the womb. Mr. Gordon frequently harangued the Junkers with plans for a new chariot based on a Cadillac chassis, but no one wanted to build it, let alone roll the thing on and off the scales. The Junkers weren't big on traditions that involved any sort of labor, and regularly clamored for the scrapping of the chariot idea altogether. There was a story that the present vehicle had been fabricated using some of the pieces from the original chariot, the one that carried the mythical Auditor who administered the IRS weigh–ins of antiquity. Few Junkers put as much stock in this legend as they did in the one about the farmer's daughter and the bicycle pump salesman.

Every year, after the weigh–in, Mr. Gordon began talking again about a new chariot, but every year the Junkers went to ground. The VW, meanwhile, sagged and rusted.

There was a great deal of preparation to be done before Mr. Gordon declared the weigh–in open. The big black tote board on the office wall had to be prepared, for one thing. The column of names of all the Junker families was scrawled there in pale yellow chalk. Space was left for a second column labeled "RAW WEIGHT," and a third column for "PPLI." It was this third column, reserved for the recording of Pounds Per Linear Inch, that ultimately determined the outcome of the weigh–in. This measure had the added advantage of allowing the children to participate without disproportionate penalty.

As Mr. Wimple labored over the tote board, Mr. Gordon herded the families and individuals into some semblance of a procession, prodding and cuffing his reluctant charges with the ceremonial scepter. Just as Mr. Gordon left off his adept bludgeoning and turned to take the heights of the assembled Junkers with his tape measure, Ms. Cochino lumbered along the line, her bloated feet slapping on the rubber soles of her sandals almost as loudly as her flesh apron slapped her dimpled thighs. "Christ, Nakomis," she lamented as she passed her neighbor, Ms. Harris, "Almost forgot what friggin' day it is."

Ms. Harris frowned and responded with a fart.

Ms. Cochino wedged herself into the line behind her husband, Calzone. "What's cookin'?" She licked her bloated lips and craned her neck to see what the Gordon family was fiddling with on the far side of the scales.

A wide–bodied woman clad in a fur sarong stirred the contents of a large stewing kettle while her six children assembled the feast tables from sheets of splintered plywood and fifty–five gallon chemical drums. The completed tables were soon heaped with thousands of grease–fried corn cakes and mountainous bowls of peanuts. The oldest Gordon boy ignited

140

the kindling around the entrée vat—a modified tanker truck. He stepped back as the flames spread to the logs and tire scraps beneath it. The water would be boiling before the weigh–in concluded. The Gordons all wore smug expressions, knowing they were exempted from weighing.

"Cal, waddya think? They gonna have norwoods for the side dish again?" Ms. Cochino wrinkled her pudgy nose and sniffed the air.

"Probably," her husband answered.

"Wonder what kind."

"Norwoods are norwoods, Griselda. Any fool knows that."

"I hate them furry bastards with kinky white hair." Griselda was one of a handful of Junkers dimly aware that norwoods weren't a single species of creature, but rather any fur bearing animal too slow or stupid to escape the slingshots and ball bats of men. She remembered her grandfather telling her a story about norwoods with different names. It was a funny tale centering on a girlish norwood named Br'er Poodle. Griselda's grandfather claimed that the term "norwood" was derived from the names of two other characters in this story, Br'er Norway Rat and Br'er Woodchuck, but it was commonly judged that Grandpa was full of shit.

"Stop yer yammerin', ya dumb ho," Cal said.

Griselda wound up and slammed a forearm into the back of her husband's thick neck. Cal belched and fell silent.

"Well, now," Mr. Gordon said peevishly, encouraging Mr. Wimple in the completion of the tables on the tote board with a jab of his scepter, "let's get the goddamn show on the road."

The weigh–in began.

The Bardol family was the first to mount the wooden platform of the chariot and sit on the stout bench. Mr. Holmes and his son, Mycroft, leaned into the tow rope and pulled the chariot onto the Scales of Plenty. They stepped aside wearily as Mr. Wimple, who had calibrated the scales a day earlier, deducted the chariot tare weight and recorded the raw result. A chorus of "Holy Toledo!" erupted from the Junkers after he had calculated and entered the Pounds per Linear Inch. "Six point six," he announced somnolently.

"Holy Toledo!"

The Holmeses wheeled the Bardol family off the scales and replaced them with the Greenstreets. Next came the Candys, the Gibrons, the Mussels, the Maddens, the Cambridges, the Clarisses and the Presleys.

The chariot collapsed after the thirteenth weighing. No one volunteered to prepare the Cadillac, so Mr. Gordon directed Mr. Wimple to recalibrate the scales and resort to the expedient of weighing the Junkers on the hoof.

At last, all of the families and individuals present had been weighed. The tote board was nearly full. Only one person remained.

"Weigh the prisoner!" Griselda roared. She referred to Ms. Jackson, the thin furrier who disrupted the weigh–in every year by refusing to participate. Ms. Jackson would stand atop the hubcap pyramid, raining insults down upon her heavier, healthier neighbors. Wielding a bull horn fashioned from a fluorescent orange construction pylon, she would mock tradition, the junk yard elders, and the weigh–in. Had she participated, she would have been selected, everyone was certain, but she was quicker than a young norwood and none of the Junkers could catch her. The laws governing the weigh–in provided that she could be captured and forcibly weighed, but only on November 30th. If she wasn't caught on that day, she would be free to go about her business until the following weigh–in.

Things would be different this year, however. Griselda had seen to that six months earlier when she had falsely accused the furrier of price gouging on the resale of norwood pelts. Shurleen Jackson had been languishing in the junk yard hoosegow ever since, awaiting justice at the hands of the plodding Junkers. Nothing in the law forbade weighing a prisoner awaiting trial; she wouldn't escape her turn this year.

"Bring out the anorexic ho!" Cal shouted. The murmur of agreement that rippled through the assemblage quickly grew to an enthusiastic chant: "Bring out the ho! Bring out the ho!"

Mr. Gordon nodded to Mr. Wimple, and the constable waddled around the corner of the office in the direction of the jail. When he returned with the prisoner the crowd fell silent.

"Impostor!" Griselda shrieked when Ms. Jackson came into view. The woman was chained at the wrists and ankles, yet walked with a proud swagger and held her head high. She had been transformed, like the Ugly Norwood in the children's story, into a stunningly beautiful Junker. Her legs were rubbery white trunks of flesh webbed with delicate blue veins, and her thick flesh apron bobbed alluringly below her furs, almost to her ankles. The Junkmen erupted with wolf whistles at the sight of her triple chins and blubbery arms.

"That ain't her!" Griselda howled. "Where is that skinny bitch? Bring her out!" She looked anxiously about for supporters, but there were none. Everyone recognized the changed features of Ms. Jackson, and all could see that the Cochino family had the lowest PPLI on the tote board. A new chant began: "Weigh her! Weigh her! Weigh her!"

Mr. Holmes and his son escorted the prisoner to the scales. Mr. Wimple recorded the weight, making certain to adjust for the manacles. He calculated carefully, using all of his stubby fingers and toes, then recorded the PPLI.

"Holy Toledo!" The Junkers shouted as one.

"Six even," the constable announced, his rubbery mouth stretched in an appreciative smile. "Half a pound over the Cochinos."

Cal was halfway to the scales for his individual weighing before Griselda began to protest. "It ain't fair! She cheated—can't you see that?"

"Six point five," Mr. Wimple shouted as Cal stepped off the scales.

The crowd roared, "Holy Toledo!"

"I think we oughtta start over," Griselda complained. "Anyone can see that bag of bones ain't no six pounder." The crowd cleared a path for her ascent to the scales. She jiggled with fear and stepped hesitantly toward the constable, then stopped. "It ain't fair!" She didn't begin moving again until Mr. Gordon drew near and delivered a flurry of blows on her mountainous shoulders with his scepter.

"Ow! Shit!" she exclaimed, scurrying up onto the scales. "Shit!" She looked imploringly at the constable and said, "How can it be, Mr. Wimple? Six months ago she was no bigger than a norwood. How can it be?"

The constable lowered his eyes and said, "Six months in jail with my wife's good cookin'll do that to a body, Ms. Cochino." He turned then and recorded the scale reading on the tote board. As he began to calculate the PPLI, a small boy broke away from the crowd and jabbed Griselda's naked leg experimentally with a plastic fork.

"Beat it, ya little shit," she hissed, kicking him in the general direction of his parents. She looked up to see that the crowd of Junkers had tightened in a semicircle around the scales. Everyone held forks and carving knives tightly in their plump fists. Their eyes shifted anxiously from the fumbling constable to the cloud of steam bubbling out of the entree vat.

Finally Mr. Wimple dragged the yellow chalk over the board with a screech that made everyone's hair stand straight up. "Four point nine!" he roared, turning to smile first at Griselda, then at Mr. Gordon. "Holy Toledo!"

"Holy Toledo!" Mr. Gordon agreed, licking his lips. "All right, folks. We're running late, so let's finish up quick."

Although the Junkers had forgotten much of the ritual, they remembered to use basting brushes and meat tenderizer. Mrs. DeLuise had two O'Cedar whisk brooms. She twirled them as proficiently as a Ninja assassin wielding nunchaku, and turned to her friend, Ms. Spandone. "Come on, Cass" she said, breathless with excitement. "Hurry up."

Griselda Cochino tottered in the center of the scales, and held out her hands desperately as the Junkers moved toward her. "It ain't fair," she said. A powerful stream of barbecue sauce spattered her face.

Old Lady Pickwick said, "Soup's on!"

The background grumble of empty stomachs sounded like distant thunder.

"It ain't fair! It ain't right!" Ms. Cochino screamed.

And then they were upon her.

THE SWIMMER WITH LUGGAGE

The stern rose swiftly as the *Concertina*'s prow dropped over a swell and into another trough. Cooper braced his feet against the stanchions and gripped the rail so tightly his knuckles showed white against the chocolate brown of his fists. He couldn't decide which was worse: the giddy ascents, or the helpless sensation of falling that followed. Cooper was determined not to lose his breakfast, but he decided that if it came up he would direct it at Doctor Weimar. The bastard just stood there like he was born to the sea—legs slightly bent, hands draped casually over the rail, thin brown hair rippling in the breeze.

"It seems a remarkably obnoxious way to die!" Weimar shouted as the stern settled. His voice was loud over the crash of water against the hull and gurgling throb of the ship's engines.

"I haven't given it much thought," Cooper responded. He wiped the perspiration from his forehead and glanced at the moisture on his fingertips.

"Well, it is, Raymond." Weimar let go the rail and crossed his arms. He moved with the tossing of the ship as though his feet were bolted to the deck. "The condemned man will be bound and equipped with goggles and underwater breathing apparatus; a weight will be attached to his feet and he will be cast into the sea one thousand feet above an active volcano. Did you know these particulars, Raymond?" Doctor Weimar grinned encouragingly and pushed his wire–rimmed glasses further up the bridge of his oily nose with a pale index finger.

Cooper exhaled and closed his eyes tightly in dismay. He wished he were strapped in a bunk below deck. "Yeah, yeah, yeah, Doc, I knew." He managed to turn his head toward the psychiatrist and grin defiantly even as the *Concertina* plunged sickeningly into a furrow of the sea.

Cooper wasn't pleased with the trip for many reasons, not the least of which were his motion sickness and his gnawing fear that the forty year old ship would break up and plummet to the sea bed. Until two months ago the *Concertina* had been a mothballed Navy container ship; she had been hurriedly refitted for the first Retribution Cruise. Cooper was reminded of her age with every creak and groan of the hull.

Weimar flashed a smile as the stern rose again; he looked forward as if trying to see over the horizon to Iceland. "Did you know," he said at length, "that this is only a shakedown cruise?"

"What do you mean?"

"A test. The condemned man will be electronically monitored to determine if the desired effect is achieved. If all goes as the government hopes, larger ships will make this cruise routinely with scores of passengers—perhaps as many as five hundred at a time. All booked for one way passage, of course." Weimar barked out a clipped, nasal laugh. "Did you think they would go to this much expense for one execution without some greater purpose?"

Cooper considered for a moment. "Like I said, Doc, I haven't given it much thought." He tried to imagine five hundred men splashing into the water at once. "You know I don't want to be here."

"But you *are* here. So am I." Weimar unbuttoned his vest and looked up at the pale gray sky, then at the rolling sea. He laughed again. His hands returned to the rail and he directed his gaze at the wake churned up by the *Concertina*'s screw. "I'm

sorry," he said. "I don't see much humor in today's activities—
it's just that I've often thought that some despicable people
should be sent directly to Hell. And that is what will soon
happen—after a fashion. It's clever, don't you think?"

Cooper said nothing.

"Retribution. Some crimes are so outrageous that mere
execution is insufficient. Punishment must be inflicted—so it
has been decided. Sending our wayward brethren to their Master
may not be possible in any real sense, but this," —the doctor
swept his arm at the expanse of gray–green water of the North
Atlantic— "this is an amusing and effective facsimile."

As Cooper listened, he clasped and unclasped his fingers
around the steel tubing of the rail, keeping time with the rise and
fall of the ship; either the sea was settling down or he was finally
adapting to the ceaseless motion. Now, if he could only adapt
to the psychiatrist's banter. Weimar was a compelling speaker;
with any sort of encouragement he would likely talk right
through the execution, so Cooper held his tongue and stared at
his shoes. Wisps of vapor scurried across the rust–scaled deck.

"Over the millennia," Weimar continued, as though
addressing medical students in the lecture hall, "many cultures
have employed natural phenomena to dispose of undesirables:
death by exposure, drowning, ingenious applications of gravity
and electricity. This, however, is unique." He nudged Cooper's
elbow until their eyes met. "Don't you agree?"

Cooper remained silent. His gaze returned to the steam
wafted over his shoes by the slight breeze.

"Of course, of course," Weimar observed. "Silent
acquiescence. That is perhaps how all of us came to be in the
same boat. Ha!" He choked off his laugh as if embarrassed at
having made an unintended pun. After a moment he continued
in a controlled voice. "I do not know exactly who developed
this scheme, but even you must admit that it is devilishly
creative."

Cooper stood as rigidly as a figure of ice. Five hundred
men.

"Initially I thought it was a rather grotesque concept, pointlessly cruel to the victim and unnecessarily expensive to society—morally and financially. But then I considered the frustration so many of our people shared over the years when sociopaths were set free on frivolous legal points, or, when convicted, imprisoned too briefly or put to death in an almost kindly manner. There was no satisfaction for anyone in the old system, save the attorneys, nor was there much justice, least of all for society or the victims.

"No, real justice, real satisfaction comes from the knowledge that the evil ones suffer at least an equal amount of agony as that inflicted on their prey. Execution will not guarantee that they will proceed to an eternity of discomfort on the Lake of Fire, however. One can never be sure of an afterlife, and that small doubt is sufficient reason to provide at least a taste of Hell before their existence is expurgated. People will sleep more contentedly tonight knowing that an evil man will have been flung over the side of this ship. Many will vividly imagine his speedy descent through the bright, cold water into the blackening depths, and the uncomfortable increase in pressure as the end nears. And the view! From daylight to profound darkness he will be drawn ever downward as if by the hand of the Master; if he remains conscious he will at last detect a faint orangish–red glow. The water temperature will rise and the glow will brighten to an incandescence, a roiling expanse of liquefied rock along the sea bed. The Lake of Fire! Even the atheists will sleep well tonight."

Cooper raised his head and glared. "You love this, don't you, Doc? You think it's just wonderful."

The distant look on Weimar's face vanished. He removed his glasses and wiped the oil from the bridge of nose with an immaculate handkerchief. He maintained his footing effortlessly; the deck's heaving had subsided as the *Concertina* moved into calmer waters. "I do not mean to appear enthusiastically morbid about this business, Raymond." He put the glasses back on and they immediately slid down his nose. The unnaturally white index finger again pushed them back into place. "It's just that I can't imagine a more poetic demise for a monster."

"Doc, you know I just want to get it over with." Cooper's chest tightened and a tickle of rage grew in his belly. "A 'mere execution' would do just fine, but since we're stuck with this" — he waved his arm at the sea and the ship— "this simulation of Hell, then it's what we'll do. You can talk about it all you want, but it won't do me any good. Does it matter how a man who kidnapped and tortured little boys is put to death? Even if the guy is evil or crazy or whatever?" Cooper clenched his teeth and breathed deeply through his nose. Tears welled in his eyes, and he found it difficult to keep his faltering voice from disintegrating into sobs. He cleared his throat before continuing. "The whole point is to get the bastard out of everyone's hair right? To make sure that he never gets a chance to hurt kids again, right?"

Weimar nodded thoughtfully and smiled. He slipped a gold watch from his vest pocket and drew back the cover with his thumb. "It will be over shortly, Raymond. It is nearly time." He closed the watch and tucked it back into his pocket. "Shall we go?"

Cooper sniffed and wiped his nose with his coat sleeve. He let go the rail and turned toward the bridge. He was trembling, he realized, and his legs were rubbery. Still, he did not stumble.

Weimar took Cooper by the elbow and walked with him toward the watchful execution party waiting silently amidships. "I remember my medical school mentor," he said, slowing to accommodate Cooper's unsteady gait, "a charmingly cynical internist named Morris Marrier. Doctor Marrier often said that life was like a swim in the ocean. One wades into the water and strikes out from shore never to return. In this quaint picture of life, one swims ceaselessly until succumbing to exhaustion. Then one's consciousness is drowned in the immensity of the sea; the struggle ends. Marrier always said that some swim purposefully and nearly effortlessly while most swim in circles or struggle to tread water. These ne'er–do–wells he called `swimmers with luggage'.

"The good Doctor Marrier never explained just what sort of luggage impeded his allegorical swimmers. Did he mean human relationships? Did he refer to material things? Do you think, Raymond, that he could have meant an anvil? Ha!" Weimar nudged Cooper as they arrived at the place of execution. He removed his glasses again and wiped the oil from his nose.

Two Federal Corrections Officers, grim young men in blue uniforms, seized the condemned man and manacled his arms behind his back. They fitted thick–lensed goggles to his face and tightened the rubber straps around his head to insure a watertight seal. Finally, the officers laced a battery pack and a surplus Navy emergency rebreathing kit to his belt, then made him lay on his side on a broad plank. The plank was slid into the "gallows"—a vintage torpedo launcher scavenged from the reserve fleet. The weapon's firing mechanism had been removed; it was now no more than a large tube mounted on a pivot just inboard of its point of balance.

Two burly guards bound the child mutilator's feet and chained them to a three hundred pound smith's anvil. They heaved the anvil to its resting place just inside the outboard end of the horizontal tube. A Lieutenant of Corrections flipped a switch and the motorized pivot mount powered to its resting place against the gunwale, extending the tube well out over the water. When the executioner pulled the release lever, the weight of the anvil would propel the torpedo launcher to a vertical position, and its contents would drop to the waves below.

Concertina's chaplain was not permitted to be present. The condemned man was allowed a final statement, however.

"The time has come, the Walrus said, to talk of many things: of shoes – and ships – and sealing–wax – of cabbages — and kings — And why the sea is boiling hot — and whether pigs have wings,'" Doctor Weimar quoted. "Have you anything to say to me, Raymond? This will be your last opportunity."

The guards forced the Navy surplus breathing tube into the psychiatrist's mouth and briskly tightened the webbing over his face, taking care not to obstruct the goggle lenses.

"Go to Hell, Doc," Cooper said. He threw back the release lever with all the force he could summon.

RHINOMANCY

"Get back in the coffin," Sergeant Carczak said the moment Troy Falco slipped from the Stryker's frontal armor to the sand. "You belong in here with us, not out looting corpses like a ghoul."

"Just gimme a minute, Sarge." Falco continued to move through the impenetrable black of the night, toward the dead Taliban patrol they'd spotted before sunset. He must be almost on top of them, for Christ's sake! In another minute he'd have their wallets and watches. They wouldn't need the stuff anymore, that was for sure. Some hunting F–16 or Apache had strafed their asses, but good. If Falco didn't gather the spoils, someone else would. So why was Carczak all bent out of shape?

"Get in the goddamn coffin." A *snick* punctuated the Sergeant's last remark as he flipped the safety lever on the Stryker's fifty caliber gun. The sound was distinct above the purr of the vehicle's idling diesel engine.

Sergeant Carczak drew back the bolt of the machine gun. *Ka–chink.*

"All right, Sarge, all right." Falco stopped moving. He knew Carczak was watching through Starlight goggles, so he turned and shuffled back toward the Stryker. "Don't shoot," he said. "I'm coming."

Suddenly the Stryker began to glow and Falco could see his shadow expanding before him. He looked over his shoulder into the blackness and saw a flicker of brilliant orange light. It pulsed like a low frequency strobe, illuminating the surrounding hillocks like fiery snow.

Falco dove for the ground even before he heard the fierce belch of the anti–tank gun. A hundred yard stretch of rocky turf erupted in blinding bursts of white flame as incoming rounds ripped toward the Stryker. Dozens of uranium slugs punched through the steel and ceramic hull of the armored vehicle. The twenty–ton machine lurched into the air and exploded. The shockwave slammed Falco into the sand.

He felt the strafing Warthog's throbbing passage through the chill air, then saw its burly fuselage and stubby wings as it swooped low over the flaming wreckage.

"*I'm American, you crazy bastards!*" Falco's shriek sounded no louder than a feeble whisper. He jerked himself to his knees and watched the exhaust nozzles of the tank killer recede into the night like a pair of glowing eyes. "*Friendly! Friendly! Friendly!*"

Purple warning flares popped up all over the southern horizon, marking the main body of the armored brigade eight klicks distant. The Warthog must have seen the signals, for it peeled off without firing again.

Falco struggled to his feet and approached the blazing hulk. The mortally wounded vehicle blossomed then like a monstrous orange flower, sprouting petals of orange smoke as secondary explosions of 30mm rounds hurled splinters in every direction.

☐

A chunk of shrapnel had severed the olfactory nerves and planted itself in Falco's cerebrum. He expected never to smell again, so he was surprised and happy when he began to detect odors several months into his recovery. The neurologists were quick to label his sensations "hysteria," citing the CAT scans and Falco's inability to correctly identify anything placed before his nose during blindfolded testing. When he sniffed gasoline, he smelled oranges or toothpaste; a whiff of ammonia registered as beef roast or shaving lotion. One doctor described it as a neurological illusion, much like the itching "phantom" limbs experienced by amputees.

Troy Falco and His Phantom Nose! At first it was amusing, but the smells grew in intensity as the months passed, and he found it increasingly difficult to concentrate. Eating became especially irksome. It was difficult to enjoy food that couldn't be smelled or tasted; impossible when flavored with bus exhaust, or the spectral fetor of a urinal. Foul wisps of bad breath, the tangy hint of cheap perfume, burning hair, the body odor taste of cooked cabbage—the things normally escaped with a turn of the head or a bit of walking—all became noisome anvils that Falco carried with him.

The physicians had no idea when—or even *if*—the phantom would subside. The one thing they *could* tell him was that no sane neurosurgeon would risk probing anywhere near the embedded shrapnel unless a life–threatening emergency arose. An operation to destroy his smell receptors was out of the question. Falco would have to live with it.

When he left the hospital he took a room at the once luxurious Hotel Kosciusko, now a seedy flop house for transients and pensioners. It was all he could afford until his disability checks began. He knew he couldn't depend upon the notoriously slow Federal bureaucracy to save him from eviction, so he decided to visit his father to try to borrow money before his own meager savings were exhausted. He didn't much like the old man, and the feeling was reciprocated, but he was confident that his war record would be enough to leverage a couple of grand from him.

☐

The stench began almost the moment he climbed aboard the bus to the suburbs. It was bad enough to gag him—like road kill, or sun–baked Afghanis. At first he thought another passenger had barfed or crapped himself, but a glance showed that he was the only rider. The stench lasted for more than ten minutes and wasn't relieved by holding his breath or opening the window.

The stench ended as abruptly as it had begun, and yielded to the sweet smell of fresh lawn clippings. He dismissed the experience as another phantom sensation and began to ponder the coming reunion with his father.

Falco walked nine blocks from the bus stop to the sprawling white ranch house, cursing the midafternoon heat all the way. He rang the bell and waited patiently, mopping sweat from his face with his shirt sleeves before ringing a second time. When no one came to the door, he tried knocking. "Pops! *Hey, Pops!* You in there?"

The old man had to be home—his prized El Dorado was parked in the drive. A quick check assured there was no one in the back yard. He circled back to the front of the house and pounded on the door for a full minute. Finally he tried the polished brass knob. It was unlocked.

Falco found his father in the living room. The old man must have had a stroke or a heart attack, judging by the way he was sprawled on his back across the coffee table. His gnarled right hand was at his throat and his head hung nearly to the floor. The dead eyes had rolled back in their sockets, and looked like mummified hard–boiled eggs. The corpse was bloated and discolored, and had obviously ripened for a week or more in the June heat. It was a testament to the old man's unceasing war against household insects that his remains weren't crawling with maggots.

"You sorry son of a bitch," was the best Falco could do by way of eulogy before entering the kitchen to rummage through the cupboards. His father's household cash was secreted in a plastic bag at the bottom of a flour tin. He pocketed the money and used the wall phone to dial '911.' At length he returned to the living room.

He toyed briefly with the idea of liberating the dead man's wallet, but decided against it. His father rarely carried more than a few bucks—not enough to risk arousing police suspicions of foul play if they saw that the corpse had been disturbed. As he gazed at the old man he realized something was wrong. Something was missing. No stink.

He couldn't smell anything identifiable at the moment, but his eyes told him that the odor in the room must be incredible. The idea of inhaling the putrescent gases of decomposing flesh set his stomach churning. He rushed outside into the fresh air, gasping and coughing.

Falco slowed his breathing and sat on the porch step to wait for the police. His thoughts turned to the old man's will. He'd been written out of it years earlier—his younger brothers would inherit everything. Those sniveling, boot–licking bastards would get it all. He looked back at the door and leveled a parting curse at his father. "You dirty, stinking, rotten—"

It was then that he realized he *had* smelled the corpse. Of course he had—half an hour earlier on the bus. What else could it have been? But how could he have smelled something thirty minutes before he was exposed to it? There was only one answer, crazy as it seemed.

He could smell the future.

That was why the noxious fumes the neurologists had wafted in his face smelled like food to him: the testing schedule at the hospital gibed with his dinner schedule. Breakfasts tasted like soap and aftershave because he always showered later in the morning. Suddenly every awful or vivid odor he could remember was linked to an experience that occurred minutes or hours later.

It wasn't a neurologic phantom, after all. He grinned, and the grin steadily expanded to a broad smile as each recollection reinforced the revelation.

□

Falco's initial excitement was reduced to despair within a week. There was no profit in his newfound talent. Much as he tried, Falco could think of no practical application for it. It was maddening. Seeing into tomorrow, hearing what was to happen, even feeling the shape of things to come might present money–making opportunities, but smelling the future was less than useless. The worst of it was that his sense of smell was sharper, more discriminating than ever. It was a curse.

Falco quickly became obsessed with controlling what he smelled. He experimented with scent–deadening substances, and found that cigarettes, booze, and cough drops dulled the sense to a tolerable degree. Soap seemed to lessen the dulling effect, so he quit bathing. He grew used to his own body stink, and decided that it helped mask undesirable scents.

After his discovery, Falco rarely ventured out into the numbing reek of the city. He left the comforting, familiar stench of his hotel room only when absolutely necessary.

☐

Falco threw back the yellowed sheets and sprang from the bed, kicking aside the litter of soiled clothes, vodka bottles and crumpled cigarette packs. He tore open the door and bolted down the corridor, wearing only his jockey shorts.

"Taylor!" He stopped at room 606 and kicked wildly at the chipped green paint of the six–panel door. Blood spurted from beneath the black semicircle of his toenail. "Taylor, you *goddamned son of a bitch!*"

The only response was a clatter and a groan.

"You know I hate cabbage, Taylor!" Falco punched the door for emphasis, leaving a black smudge. "Don't cook it, man. You cook that shit today and I'll be back with my bat. You hear me?" He pounded the door with his fist a final time and returned to his room.

Taylor would cook cabbage for lunch. Nothing would change that. Falco could beat him to death with his aluminum

Bombat and that cabbage would still get cooked. Maybe the police investigators would cook it while dusting for prints. Maybe it would cook itself, but somehow it would get cooked. All he knew for sure was what he'd discovered two months after his nose began to function again: when he smelled something, it happened.

Falco slammed the door and lit a Lucky Strike, letting the thick smoke curl slowly from his nostrils. He stepped to the window and leaned against the sash. The gray March sky was filtered to a sickly brown by the film of tar on the glass. Bare–limbed saplings in Division Park danced to the rhythms of the cold wind that whirled in from Lake Erie. It was snowing again. Already he felt control slipping away as a growing storm of odors assailed him: car exhaust, street salt, the algae and sewage of the lake. He smoked the cigarette down to a stub and butted it on the sill.

At two–thirty he dressed in jeans and a wrinkled t–shirt plucked from the heap on the floor and tugged a pair of tattered sneakers over his bare feet. He buttoned his rancid pea coat on the way out the door. After plodding down five flights of stairs to the lobby he remembered the money. A panicky search of his pockets produced the V.A. check. It wasn't much, but it was enough to resupply him with Luckies, eucalyptus lozenges, and vodka, the three things he needed to suppress his sense of smell—enough to keep him sane for another month.

The momentary fear of losing the check had done nothing to take the edge off his burgeoning anxiety. His grimy hands trembled as he lit his last cigarette and dropped the empty pack on the floor. He stepped out onto Washington Street and headed for the bank as quickly as his rubbery legs would carry him. He cursed himself for procrastinating. Sick or not, he should have made this trip two days earlier. The flu that wracked his body was nothing compared to the torment of the smells that lay ahead.

The wind stung his face and drove snow into his coat. He pulled the wool collar up and tucked his greasy hair beneath it, hunching his shoulders so his unshaved chin slipped into the coat like a turtle's head retreating to its shell. He took a last long drag on the cigarette and flicked the butt into the grimy snow bank along the curb.

He tried to gauge the fever with his palm. His forehead was still hot, but better or worse, he couldn't tell. As he withdrew his hand his touch lingered on the scar. The shrapnel had punctured his skull like a knife thrust through a tin can, yet all that remained of the wound was a dimpled vertical furrow and the two horizontal creases left by the surgeon's scalpel.

He turned up Main Street and pulled his pea coat tightly about him as the change of direction brought him into the teeth of the wind. Half a block from his destination a couple of faint yet familiar odors emerged from the mélange of city stench. The stronger of the two was an acrid, sulfurous smell that reminded him of burned matches. But it wasn't matches. The other was as much a taste as a smell—a salty sensation at the back of his tongue, as though he'd sucked on a fistful of pennies. He didn't strain himself trying to identify them—he knew he'd find out soon enough. He always did.

The penny taste had become annoyingly intense by the time he swung through the revolving brass doors of the bank, while the burned match odor began to fade. He took his place in line and waited for a teller. When his turn came, he bolted to the bronze cage and shoved the check and his identification card at the pretty teller waiting there. He shifted his weight from foot to foot and drummed his fingers on the marble counter as the young woman dealt out the crisp, green notes. She counted the money with agonizing slowness. Three times. Falco counted it twice himself before stuffing it into his coat pocket. He hurried toward the door, but stopped suddenly a few strides from the cage. He had recognized the fading smell. Gunsmoke.

Christ, he'd whiffed it often enough in the Army that he should have known what it was immediately. Such a smell in a bank could mean only one thing. And he didn't like the idea of witnessing a bank robbery.

He was sure the hold–up hadn't taken place yet—if it had, the place would be closed and swarming with cops. That left only two possibilities: the bank would be robbed while he was in it, or he would return after the robbery went down. Since he had no reason to come back to the bank for another four weeks, it was a pretty safe bet he'd be around for the fireworks. Hell, he *smelled* it.

What troubled him as he stood undecided between the growing line of customers and the marble counter was the possibility that he might not merely witness the robbery, but fall victim to it. If the people who were going to pull the job were already inside, they had probably seen him stuff the wad of bills inside his coat. He didn't think a stick–up man worth his salt would pass up such an opportunity.

If the robbers got away with Falco's cash, it could not be replaced. He'd have to spend the next month in a shelter or beg for money. Without his "medications," either option would be an olfactory nightmare. Sure as shit he wouldn't get money for vodka and cigarettes from Catholic Charities or the Salvation Army. A check, on the other hand, could be replaced, perhaps even in a day or two. All he had to do was get the check back and he'd be safe.

His decision made, he whirled and strode back to the teller, cutting ahead of the old woman who was next in line. "I want my check back!"

"Hey," the silver–haired woman tapped him on the shoulder. "You had your turn!"

Falco turned and glared at her. "Shut up, bitch."

She gasped and stepped backward.

"Sir," the teller said in a stern voice, "you'll have to go to the end of the line."

Falco faced the cage. "Look, take your money." Whatever was going to happen was going to happen soon. He fumbled in his coat for the bills. His voice was a wavering croak. "I need my check back."

"I'm afraid you'll have to wait your turn."

"Yeah, wait your turn," the dozen or so waiting customers chorused.

"I said *shut up!*" Falco spun around and shoved the old woman toward the head of the line. He turned back to the bronze cage and tried to bring his voice under control. "You don't understand! I need my check back."

The teller ignored him, looking instead toward the door. "Bob? Bob! We have a problem here."

The security guard posted there was already underway.

Falco threw his head back and rolled his eyes, laughing hysterically as the man approached. The guard, a middle–aged black man with a crown of gray hair and a pot belly, looked like a retired middle linebacker. Falco tried to reason with the teller one last time. "You don't understand, you dumb bitch. Here's my money, give me my check back!"

A strong hand clutched his upper arm. He shrugged it off and stuffed the money back into his coat. "All right, all right."

"Come on, pal." The guard grabbed Falco again and started dragging him toward the door. "I think you'd better find another bank." The man wrinkled his nose and sneered at Falco's unkempt appearance. "Try taking a bath first though. Come on." He tightened his grip and tugged harder.

"Okay, I'm coming," Falco said. He smiled helplessly at the angry, disgusted faces of the customers waiting in line as the guard towed him away from the teller's cage.

Then he saw the robbers: three young black men lounging around a writing desk against the marble façade of the far wall. There they were, three hoods wearing Raiders coats, collars buttoned up over their chins, and wool ski masks pulled low on their foreheads. What reason other than robbery would three guys like that have for loitering in the bank? Christ, it was obvious. Couldn't the guard see it? Couldn't he *smell* it?

"There's going to be a robbery," he hissed out of the corner of his mouth. He planted his feet on the mosaic floor.

"What?" The guard swung his round black face toward Falco and loosened his grip.

"Those guys over there" —Falco indicated the three men with a jerk of his head— "are going to rob the bank."

A look of alarm swept over the guard's face. He glanced at the three young men then shot Falco a sarcastic smile. "I don't think so."

"You don't understand. I can smell it."

"Okay, you crazy bastard." The guard grabbed Falco tightly with both hands and hauled him toward the door with renewed determination. "You're *outta* here!"

Falco panicked as his sneakers skittered across the floor. It was about to happen and here was this fat fool playing right into the robbers' hands. He just wanted to go back to his room, away from these smells, these people. He wanted to go home and get drunk and smoke and watch television. But the guard was giving him the bum's rush. Well, goddamnit, nobody was going to take money from Falco. *Nobody.*

He unsnapped the cover on the guard's holster with his free hand and withdrew the 9mm semi–auto. The guard tried to grab the gun, but Falco landed a vicious kick on his shin and stepped away. The man groaned and dropped to a crouch, clutching his leg.

"There's going to be a robbery, you idiot," Falco said, drawing back the slide to feed a round into the chamber. He pivoted and waved the pistol at the three thugs. *"You!"*

One of the tellers screamed.

"He's got a gun!" someone else yelled.

The bank echoed with footsteps and shouting. Falco saw the line of customers tumble to the floor like falling dominoes. The three robbers dropped to the floor as well, and cowered around the legs of the writing stand with their arms coiled protectively about their heads. Falco hadn't expected this, and was uncertain what to do next. He aimed the gun from one to another and back again.

"Drop the goddamn gun!"

The deep voice had come from behind him. At first he thought it was one of the holdup men, but as he looked slowly over his shoulder he saw it was the guard. The man knelt in a combat stance, his pant leg bunched up over an ankle holster.

His elbows were locked and his hands overlapped in a vise–like grip on a .38 snub–nosed revolver. It was aimed at Falco.

"Drop it!"

"You don't understand," Falco said, and swung his body around to face the guard. In his exasperation he forgot to lower the weapon in his hand.

The guard rapidly squeezed off five shots. The slugs slammed into Falco's chest like blows from a club. He lurched backward a few steps and dropped to his knees, then fell forward, smashing his teeth as his face met the marble floor. He scarcely felt the bolt of pain that shot up his arm when the guard kicked the gun away from him. He blinked away tears and saw a forest of legs encircling him. His ears hummed with the murmur of voices.

"Crazy bastard thought my son and his friends were bank robbers. He took my gun. You saw—I had to shoot him."

"You did the right thing, Bob."

"Christ, is he dead?"

"Call an ambulance."

"The cops are on their way."

Falco drew his hands under his shoulders and tried get up. As he raised his head, thick strands of gore stretched from his mouth to a growing crimson pool. He knew when he saw the blood why he had tasted pennies. But the salty copper flavor was already gone, replaced by something new.

Falco closed his eyes and settled back to the floor. Gentle hands rolled him over onto his back, and someone placed a makeshift pillow under his head. He tried to ask for a cigarette, but could only cough. The effort sent a bolt of agony through his chest. And the new smells were beginning to bother him. If only he could stop the smells.

"You'll be okay, pal. The ambulance is on the way."

Falco smiled wearily and thought of what Sergeant Carczak had said so long ago. *You belong in here with us.* The Stryker commander had been right, of course. Far better to die in a blazing instant of obliteration than face what his nose told him lay ahead.

The air in Troy Falco's future was redolent of spring rain and humus, dank confinement, and the tangy breath of worms. Cool, rotting flesh and the gases of decay.

THE CALL OF TAWISKARO

Terri Destino flinched at the cracking sound and dropped to a crouch as the ice shifted beneath her. She pushed off the hard surface with her gloved hands and turned to look for her friends. The tiny peninsula of ice on which she was standing had broken free and was moving out into the middle of the upper Niagara. She dug the teeth of her hockey skates into the ice and bolted for shore, only to pull up short at the last instant in a shower of ice chips and water. It was too late. The band of dark green between her and the sheet ice was already too wide to risk leaping. Even if she knew how to swim, it would be impossible in tightly laced skates and heavy winter clothing.

Buckhorn Island had receded to a pale gray ribbon surmounted by a black wall of trees before it occurred to her to scream. "Joey! *Joeeiiieee!*"

The black stick figures skating along the white strip of ice converged at water's edge. She cupped her hands at her mouth and screamed again.

Someone broke away from the group and moved quickly toward the trees. That had to be Joey. Terri could just make out his red wool cap as he scurried up the embankment and disappeared into the woods. Joey would get help, but could anyone reach her quickly enough? It would take him a good ten minutes to get to the Thruway toll barrier. After that it might take an hour to launch a boat or send a helicopter to save her. She looked downriver.

A cloud of silver mist rose from the water in the distance and merged with slate gray clouds. The falls weren't much more than a couple of miles away. The current in this part of the river was maybe two or three miles per hour. *Knots*, she thought. *On the water you say knots. The closer you get to the gorge, the faster you move.* She'd learned in school that the river got up to twenty knots before it dropped into the gorge. There wasn't much time.

The north shore was black with the silhouettes of factories twinkling with red and amber lights—a forest of smoke stacks and cooling towers topped with pulsing aircraft beacons. A few cars crept along the parkway, but late on a Sunday afternoon with a March storm brewing those drivers who had to be out would be concentrating on the treacherous road ahead of them. No one would cast more than a curious glance at the river, and even if anyone did, Terri knew she would be tough to see through the fuzzy curtain of falling snow.

Terri saw an ice breaker tied up at the cement quay below the twin gate towers of the Power Authority water intakes. The moment she noticed it she began hopping about on her skate blades, waving her arms wildly, but the ice floe listed and she was soon thrashing about in shin–deep water. She scrambled backward to the center of her precarious raft. The ice slowly righted itself. Gathering courage, she stood again to shout, but knew immediately that no one was on the boat to hear; the pilot house windows were dark.

Terri slumped to her knees and huddled in her ski jacket with her hands tucked beneath her arms. She scarcely noticed the dull pain where the skate blades jabbed her buttocks. Her legs were already numbed by the icy water that had soaked through her jeans, and her feet ached with cold.

The wind picked up, hooting around her as it drove sheets of wet snow over the water. The muffled cry of a gull came from above and Terri looked up, wondering why a bird would be so stupid as to fly in this weather. Snowflakes melted on the lenses of her glasses; she saw nothing but a gray fog of snow, and the gull's shrill squawks sounded like mocking laughter.

"You're right, bird," she called out. "I'm the dumb one."

You can fly home, she thought, but I'm stuck here—for a little while, anyway. She shivered and exhaled a wisp of vapor. What had drawn her out onto the thin ice? One minute she was skating along the shore, and the next she was out here. It was as if an old friend had called to her, and she had come without thinking.

"Tawiskaro." She said the name in a panicky little girl voice and looked around quickly to make certain she was alone. A dark blur rushed at her out of the gloom, and she ducked. It was only a gull—perhaps the same one she'd heard just a moment before. The creature slowed and hovered in a whirl of snow, then settled to the ice with a noisy flap of its wings.

Terri swung her arm at the gull, but it was out of reach. "Shoo!"

The bird merely cocked its head and stared, as if to say, "This is my turf. *You* shoo!"

Terri met its gaze and thought for a moment that it had actually spoken to her. Its beak was tightly closed, yet she'd heard something. She listened hard and could still hear it. A low, steady voice, just above a whisper—the distant sound of falling water. Or was it Tawiskaro calling to her?

Terri had never really believed in Tawiskaro, but she was almost forced to believe in him now. Something had called her out onto the ice—why not him? As she stared at the gull she wanted to believe in the Guardians, too. "Are you one?"

The creature's tiny black eyes blinked. It answered with a hoarse cry then spread its wings and leapt into the air, flying rapidly north.

The cloud of mist downriver was indistinguishable now from the falling snow. A broad shadow emerged from the pale gray swirl downstream: black rocks and skeletal trees, the span of a steel arch bridge. Goat Island. Terri knew that the rapids began at the eastern tip of the island separating the American Fall from the Horseshoe Fall. That meant there wasn't much time.

The river began to gurgle around her then as the channel narrowed and humps of rock rose to break the surface. Terri leaned forward, bracing herself with her hands as the ice bobbed into rougher water. She closed her eyes tightly and tried to wish herself home into bed, snug under her pink comforter at the end of a nightmare. But when she opened her eyes, she was still on the ice, moving ever faster toward the fall. "Mama," she whispered, and began to cry.

☐

The cop was a much better teacher than Mr. Carabetta. Jimmy Carabetta was a douche. His idea of seventh grade social studies was to read aloud from the textbook like he was addressing a flock of idiots. The book was lousy to begin with, but it was unbearable to hear him read dull chapter after dull chapter in his weak, nasally voice. When he wasn't reciting from the book, he made the class watch film strips—a kind of slide show accompanied by a narrator on a scratchy record. Even Terri's mother said film strips were an ancient teacher's aide, but Carabetta thought they were great.

He was a douche, all right, but he did one cool thing: guest speakers. All sorts of people from outside the school came into his classroom to talk. He never took the class anywhere, but he'd bring anybody in. Like this cop.

"Sergeant Greene," Richie Laszewski croaked, "are you allowed to scalp murderers when you catch them?" The question trailed off to a snigger and Richie cupped a hand over his pimply face. Mr. Carabetta frowned. The other boys choked off laughs and looked innocently at the ceiling.

The big cop threw back his head and laughed. "No special privileges because I'm an Indian, kid," he said after a moment. "The Parks Police mostly hand out tickets for speeding and

172

littering, and we keep people from hurting themselves. We don't run across many killers. Except the river."

The Tuscarora stood with legs spread and hands clasped behind his back. With his crisply pressed navy–on–gray uniform, he reminded Terri of her older brother, Curtis, the way he'd looked and acted after he came back from Iraq. Like a man—serious, but always ready to laugh.

Sergeant Greene plucked the broad–brimmed Stetson from his head and ran his long fingers through his spiky black hair. He sat down on a steam radiator near the windows and nodded toward the blue–green water just across Buffalo Avenue. The class followed his gaze. "That river has murdered more people than any serial killer who ever lived. Just remember what I told you." The cop was stern again. He'd meant what he'd said about water safety.

Terri wondered if he was as good a cop as he was a teacher. Even the boys had hung on his every word as he talked about things they'd had lectures on a hundred times before: drugs, cars, fireworks, water. Anyone could see that he knew what was what, and that he cared. Especially when he talked about the river.

"Now," he said. "Who can tell me why it's so dangerous out there?"

"The currents," Santo Manessi answered immediately. "The falls."

"You listened! Good. Everything I said is true, but," — Sergeant Greene's deep voice was suddenly soft and conspiratorial— "there are other reasons why the river is dangerous."

Terri hunched forward in her chair; she could tell by the way he looked over either shoulder, that he was about to tell a ghost story. Her father did it just that way. With the Indian summer sun beating through the windows it seemed more like August than late October, but something in the cop's voice and the way he shifted his eyes from one face to the next created a chill of anticipation that had all the feeling of Halloween.

173

"Before the Tuscaroras lived here," he began, "there was a tribe called the Onguiaarhas. They're all gone now, and it is said that they died because they worshipped a demon."

The class was deathly silent. No paper wads or whispered jokes. Just a bunch of kids gazing in rapt attention at the storyteller. Even Mr. Carabetta, who had earlier seemed impatient for his guest to finish, was attentive.

Sergeant Greene scanned the faces before him with his twinkling black eyes and nodded, as if satisfied that all were listening. "The Onguiaarhas believed that Hino, the thunder god, lived in a crystal cave beneath the falls. Hino was a kind spirit who despised evil. He created the rains with the mist from his thundering waters, and the Onguiaarhas thanked him for nourishing their corn by sending him one of their children at harvest time. Every Autumn the chief selected the tribe's most beautiful young girl as a bride for Hino. It was a great honor for the girl chosen, because she would spend an eternity with the wonderful spirit.

"The lucky girl dressed in the finest white doeskins and the tribe had a grand wedding party. Then she was carried to the river in a white birch canoe filled with corn and berries and beaver pelts—all gifts for the thunder god. The girl then paddled down into the rapids and disappeared over the fall and into Hino's mists."

"The Maid of the Mist," Hollis Winkfield said.

Terri glared at the back of the boy's head. Hollis was a douche, too. Everybody knew the legend of the Maid of the Mist. The tour boats in the gorge were named after her.

"Yes," Sergeant Greene confirmed. "But there's more to the story. One year the rains failed and the harvest was bad, so the tribe offered two sacrifices. The next year they had another bad harvest, and they tried giving Hino three brides, but their luck remained poor. It wasn't until they offered four sacrifices that the rains returned and their corn flourished again. Four maids, it seemed, were now needed to satisfy the thunder god.

"The Onguiaarha began to worry. They knew that their daughters were the tribe's future: if they gave all their daughters

174

to the thunder god, there would one day be no mothers. Without mothers, there would be no more Onguiaarhas. They tried to speak with Hino through their prayer stones. When he didn't answer they donned crooked–mouth false–face masks and conjured the whirlwind spirit, Hadu'i. They begged him to convince Hino to be content with fewer of their children, but Hadu'i could not help them. He told them that the thunder god had gone away to right some great wrong in the north, and that the evil trickster, Tawiskaro, had come to dwell in the crystal cave.

"They were horrified, for they knew all about Tawiskaro. He was a powerful demon who fed upon human souls. Every year he needed at least four, though he would devour as many souls as came to him. But he always demanded four. If he didn't get enough to eat, he made sure no one else did.

"The wise old Clan mothers told the chief what had happened and begged him to stop the sacrifices, but he would not. He and the rest of the Onguiaarhas were already enchanted by the trickster. The old women could only pray for Hino's return.

"A few years later, the French explorers and soldiers came and brought terrible diseases that weakened the tribe. Finally, in a war with the neighboring Senecas, the Onguiaarhas were wiped out. All that remains of them is their name, which we now pronounce *Niagara*. Hino never returned, but it is said that Tawiskaro never left."

Sergeant Greene stood. He tugged the gray hat back onto his head and frowned. "That's the real reason the river is so dangerous—because Tawiskaro calls at least four people to him every year. He doesn't care if they are boys or girls or men or women—so long as they have souls. And there are many who hear his call. Even though they don't know who he is, they hear his call and they come.

"I'll bet some of you have heard him. Have you ever walked across the Rainbow Bridge and looked down into the gorge? Have you heard him then, asking you to fly to him, climb the railing and float down to his mists?"

The boys in the front row nodded and exchange wide–eyed glances.

"Have you ever stood at Prospect Point and felt the power? Have you had to turn away or leave for fear you'd jump? That's him. That's Tawiskaro calling."

Several kids raised their hands to ask questions. Terri raised her hand, too, and immediately wondered why she had done so.

"Yes?" Sergeant Greene said, pointing at Terri. "Yes, you."

His eyes held hers with an unblinking gaze, as though he were looking into her thoughts. She blushed and tore off her heavy plastic glasses. Her eyes dropped to the blurred outline of the thick frames in her hands. She tried to moisten her lips but her tongue was dry. "But," she whispered, then more loudly, "but look at all the people who are rescued. Why does this Taska . . ."

"Tawiskaro."

"Why does he let them get away?"

"Because he only eats the souls of those who answer his call. And he fears Hino's Guardians."

"Guardians?"

"After the Onguiaarhas were gone, the Senecas, and later the Tuscaroras, chose Guardians to make sure that none of their daughters were sacrificed to Tawiskaro. The Guardians turned away those who answered his call. Even so, they could not stop everyone, and it was a lucky year when the demon ate only four souls. He always gets at least four. The clan mothers say that there are still Guardians, and that there will always be at least one with the courage to fight Tawiskaro until Hino returns."

"Who are they?" one of the boys asked.

Terri pushed her glasses back on and raised her head.

Sergeant Greene was still looking at her. He smiled. "Only the clan mothers can say."

☐

The rapids were just ahead. They made a sound like sinister applause, a continuous clapping of ten thousand pairs of hands. The ice moved quickly toward the narrow channel north of Goat Island, heading directly for the American Fall. The water wasn't too rough yet, but that would change once Terri passed the tip of the island. There the rock outcroppings and shelves began to churn the river. She would be dead in a few minutes.

"No." Terri rose suddenly and dragged the sleeve of her ski jacket across her nose. She was now more angry than afraid, determined not to just sit on a slab of ice and die without trying something. The thought of ending up dead in the gorge with a nose full of snot infuriated her. "No!"

There would be a couple of chances to save herself once the white water started, but she'd have to make those chances. She stripped off her gloves and threw them into the river. Her legs ached and groaned in protest as she brought her feet out in front of her. She began plucking at the skate laces, but the cotton strips were stiff with ice. Her numbed fingers couldn't manage the knots so she hammered them soft with her skate blades. It seemed to take forever, but the laces were untied long before the rapids. It was a small success, yet it strengthened her resolve. She was *doing* something.

"I'm not dying today, Tawiskaro," she shouted, then kicked the skates into the whirling black water and lay on her back. "I'm not going with you, douche!" Using her heels and elbows to draw herself feet first to the edge of the ice, she plunged her legs into the water and began kicking, trying to propel herself into the shallows. The water was so cold that it registered in her brain not as a sensation of temperature but as a bone–jarring impact or a strong jolt of electricity. After a dozen strokes her legs felt dead from the knees down and she was no closer to safety for her efforts. She dragged herself back to the center of the ice and tried to rub the circulation into the frozen limbs— she'd need them to jump to a rock or leap for a handhold beneath the bridges. The ice pitched forward then and she had to lay flat to keep from going into the water. The rapids had begun.

Terri's heart rose to her throat. She plunged into a deep trough and rose again as the river surged over the rocks. Caught in the heavy rapids, she was too far from the island shallows or the north shore to do anything now except ride. The water slammed into rocks all about her, sending up sheets of spray that mixed with the wind–tossed snow to form a crust of ice on her clothing. The river roared and hissed like a disapproving audience as she moved toward the calmer water only to be repelled by an outcropping of shale and sent back into the torrent. Black, teeth–like stones knocked chunks from the ice floe until it was half its original size, yet she managed to stay on by laying flat with her arms and legs spread desperately wide.

The worst of the rapids was the stretch between the bridges, then there was relatively calm water for the last few hundred feet before the drop into the gorge. She thought there was a chance to snag a cable or pipe under one of the bridges, but she couldn't see anything like that yet. Her tiny raft rose and fell like a carnival ride, yawing and pitching. Beads of water spattered her glasses, making it difficult to see anything clearly.

She was looking for something to grab when something swooped down between her and the broad steel span of the American Rapids Bridge. At first she thought it was Tawiskaro coming to take her to his cave. It was something big, swinging on the end of a line that rose through the snow to . . . a helicopter! Now that she saw the flash of the aircraft's running lights she could distinguish the brisk slap of its rotors from the roar of the river.

The object that had dropped in front of Terri was a man dangling from a rope, skipping toward her over the gray crests of black waves. Too fast, she thought. She was sure he would knock her off the ice. At the last instant he extended his arm and moved his fist quickly up and down. He disappeared above and behind Terri as she shot under the American Rapids Bridge, into the bad water.

The ride became wilder. Soaked and bitterly cold, she somehow managed to cling to the ice, perhaps out of sheer fury: the idiot on the rope had distracted her, and she'd missed her chance to grab anything under the bridge. The ice dropped sickeningly over a stone shelf and bobbed into smoother water. She immediately looked ahead to the Goat Island Bridge, searching its stone arches for something to grab.

The man on the rope was with her again. He'd come up from behind this time. She didn't hear the helicopter or see its lights, but she felt his boot slap hard on the ice and saw him skitter by out of the corner of her eye. She ignored him, concentrating instead on the bridge.

Her limbs shrieked with pain as she rolled to her hands and knees. She saw nothing to grab as the bridge passed overhead. The falls could be heard now above the bellow of the rapids, a deep, uninterrupted "*AAAAAAAAAHHHHHHHHHHHHHHH.*"

The voice of Tawiskaro.

The channel broadened after the bridge, and its surface flattened to a rippling black. The water here was only three or four feet deep, but moving so quickly that even a powerful man could not stand against it. There would be no wading today. No leaping, either, Terri saw as her raft selected a course midway between Prospect Point and Robinson Island. The sound of the rapids receded and the voice of Tawiskaro grew to a steady roar.

Something hit Terri from behind and knocked her to her elbows, then jerked her back to a kneeling position. She looked over her shoulder, expecting to see the demon. It wasn't Tawiskaro at all, but Sergeant Greene clutching the collar of her coat. He struggled to balance on the ice while squirming out of his rescue harness. As he drew the padded loop down to Terri, her hands rose with agonizing slowness to grab it.

The cop put his arm around her and lifted, but the helicopter rose suddenly in the turbulent air and pulled the line too high. She managed to grab the harness with one hand but knew she would never have the strength to clamber into it. Sergeant Greene must have known it too, for he reached up under the back of his coat and whipped out a pair of handcuffs.

"This will hurt," he shouted. He slapped one of the manacles onto Terri's left wrist and pressed it down tight.

She gasped with the pain, but immediately understood what he intended and brought her other hand up. He drew the chain through the loop of the harness and attached the remaining manacle to her right wrist. Without warning the line went taut and Terri's arms were jerked straight up. Twin bolts of agony shot from wrists to shoulders as her feet left the ice. She fought to keep her eyes locked with the cop's.

The harness was well out of his reach. His short black hair danced in the wind as he looked up at her. "You'll need this, *Skada'gea!*" His shout was a feeble whisper beneath the thunder of the falls and the roar of the helicopter. He pulled something from around his neck and stuffed it into her frozen sock, then he stuck his arm out and extended his thumb.

The pain was incredible as the helicopter lurched upward and moved toward Prospect point, but Terri resisted the urge to close her eyes and scream. Instead she watched Sergeant Greene.

He turned toward the fall and rode the ice like a surfer. Standing in a half crouch, he spread his arms wide as if to balance himself or grapple with something. The helicopter moved away and he shrank to a black silhouette in the whirling snow. Just as he reached the brink a dense mist consolidated out of the snow and spray around him, a specter that swept up from the gorge like a reaching hand. It closed on him, and he was gone.

The helicopter accelerated then and Terri began to spin like a top, around and around, faster and faster. She closed her eyes.

☐

It was a green stone in a silver setting. The spring sunshine pouring through the windows danced brilliantly off its facets as Terri turned it in her fingers for the hundredth time. Was it an emerald? Maybe quartz. She knew it was important because giving it to her was the last thing the cop did before dying. Just why it was so important she intended to find out. But it was only one of many nagging questions she had. How had Sergeant

Greene known where to find her? Did the gull somehow tell him? How had he commandeered a sightseeing helicopter? Why was he anywhere near the falls on his day off? She frowned and pulled the stone up to eye level, drawing the leather neck thong taut.

"It would be wise to keep that hidden," someone said.

Terri started at the voice and tucked the stone back down the neck of her pajamas. She hastily pulled the scratchy yellow blanket up to her chin and turned to the door. An old woman was standing just inside the room. Her brown face was a mask of wrinkles.

"Hi," Terri said. It wasn't even close to visiting hours and this woman was obviously not a nurse or a hospital volunteer.

"You're Terri Destino." The woman stepped forward and drew her blue cotton dress up behind her knees then sat on the edge of the bed. She wore a belt of linked turquoise stones set in silver. A pair of matching rings dangled from her ears. A thick braid of silver hair swept down over her right shoulder and rested on her chest.

"Yes. Who are you?"

The woman's glistening black eyes all but disappeared in webs of wrinkled flesh as she smiled. "I am Susie Greene."

Terri blushed. She should have known this was a relative of the cop. "You're Sergeant Greene's mother?"

"No, little one," Susie Greene chuckled. "But I thank you for the compliment. Bobby was my grandson."

"Was he a Guardian?" Terri blurted the question and felt even more embarrassed. She might have told this woman how wonderful her grandson had been—how brave and selfless. Instead she wanted to have her nagging questions answered.

Susie Greene didn't answer, but reached deftly under the blanket and into Terri's pajamas. She withdrew the stone and held it gently in her palm. "He gave you this, did he not?"

"Is it yours?" Terri glanced at the stone and was suddenly afraid. "Have you come to take it back? Are *you* a Guardian?"

Susie Greene snorted and released the gem. Her eyes widened and she chuckled again, slapping her thigh briskly. "No, *Skada'gea*, I am a clan mother. *You* are the Guardian."

Terri stared at her blankly.

"Did you hear? Do you understand?" The old woman's black eyes looked deeply into Terri's, just as her grandson's had. The gaze was powerful, magical.

Terri thought for a moment, then nodded. Yes, she *was* a Guardian. She'd thumbed her nose at Tawiskaro, hadn't she? "What is `Skaga . . . ?' "

"*Skada'gea*. It means 'mist bird.'"

"Skada'gea," Terri repeated. She liked the name. It fit.

"You have much to learn, little one." The old woman was smiling again.

There was so much that Terri didn't know, about Hino, and Tawiskaro—about everything—that she wasn't sure where to begin. But if she was to be a Guardian, she had to start learning somewhere. She returned Susie Greene's smile. "Can you teach me how to swim?"

The old woman's eyes widened, then she tossed back her head and laughed.

Publishing History

ABOUT THE AUTHOR

T. W. Kriner resides in Williamsville, New York with his wife and two cats.